"*THIS ADAPA* - HE
WHO HAS BROKEN
THE WINGS OF
THE MIGHTY
SOUTH WIND

YOU MUST

SEND HIM

TO ME!"

GREAT WORLD BOOKS ™
COLLECTION - VOL # 1

# ADAPA's

# ASCENT

## A Myth of Man
## & IMMORTALITY

ADAPA'S ASCENT
A Myth of Man & IMMORTALITY
Translation © 2019 E. d'Araille.
First published in the *Great World Books*™
*Collection* by LIVING TIME™ Global 2020.
Pbk Edition © 2020, LIVING TIME™ BOOKS.

A CIP (Cataloguing in Publication) Data Record
for this title is available from The British Library.

ISBN 978-1-908936-07-3

The Essays 'Adapa's Ascent'
and 'The Birth of Fiction'
© 2019 Edouard d'Araille.

LIVING TIME™ BOOKS
livingtimebooks.com

# ADAPA's

# ASCENT

## A Myth of Man & IMMORTALITY

translated into
**English Verse**
*by*

# Edouard d'ARAILLE

Dedicated to
All my Children

**Natalya  Mikaela**
**Matilda  Izraela**
**Talyana  Samuela**

And the Children
of the Future

## EDITORIAL NOTE

Please take note that, at all points throughout this publication, the poem at its heart is referred to as *Adapa's Ascent*, whereas the sum total of all the cuneiform tablets on which it is based are referred to as 'Adapa'. It is vital to distinguish between the poetic version that is presented here and the group of original textual sources that it attempts to present to a modern audience. The name of *this* work is italicized, wherever it is referred to, while the cluster of Adapa sources are at all points labelled collectively as 'Adapa', in single speech marks. Equally, if the original Gilgamesh stories are being referred to, the body of original sourceworks are referred to as 'Gilgamesh' (equally in single speech marks); if a particular translation of 'Adapa' or 'Gilgamesh' is being mentioned, then the translator is specifically named. What is presented in this volume is only a speculative translation of 'Adapa' and it must be clearly distinguished from the originals. As far as capitalization is concerned, some of this is done for the sake of emphasizing core distinctions, such as 'God' or 'Goddess' having an initial capital while 'human' or 'man' does not, 'Immortality' opposed to 'mortality', etc. Though standard adherence to grammatical capitalization is generally respected, where a point being made can be appropriately underlined through the use of initial capitals for specific words, then some degree of poetic license is taken. —

# PAGEFINDER

PUBLISHER'S NOTE ..................................................... iv

THE BIRTH OF FICTION - Edouard d'Araille .......................... ix

ACKNOWLEDGEMENTS ....................................................... lxxi

# ADAPA's ASCENT
## A Myth of Man & IMMORTALITY

0. *Prologue of Destiny* ........................................... 3

I. ADAPA of ERIDU ................................................. 4

II. UPON the WIDE SEA ............................................. 7

III. ADAPA'S DESCENT .............................................. 9

IV. The POWER of WORDS ........................................... 10

V. *"BRING THAT MAN HERE!"* ...................................... 13

VI. The PROPHECIES of ENKI *Part the 1st* ....................... 15

VII. BY ROYAL COMMAND ............................................. 19

VIII. The PROPHECIES of ENKI *Part the 2nd* ..................... 20

**IX.** JOURNEY to the GREAT ABOVE ........................... 22

**X.** In the PALACE of KING ANU ........................................ 25

**XI.** *"WHY?"* ........................................................................ 28

**XII.** = GIFTS IMMORTAL = ........................................... 29

**XIII.** BANISHED from the HEAVENS ......................... 32

**XIV.** - DEAR ENKI - ......................................................... 34

**XV.** *"WHO AMONG GODS?"* ......................................... 37

**XVI.** ADAPA'S ASCENT ................................................. 38

**XVII.** 'SO BE IT' ............................................................... 40

**00.** *Epilogue The Invocation* .......................................... 41

## APPENDICES OF SUPPLEMENTARY MATERIAL

**A.** CHARACTER GLOSSARY ...................................... 49

**B.** 'ADAPA'S ASCENT' - Recreating an Ancient Classic .......... 53

**C.** THE SOURCES OF *ADAPA'S ASCENT* ................................. 157

**D.** TRANSLATION SKETCH OF A SUMERIAN TEXT ............ 169

**E.** SUGGESTIONS FOR FURTHER READING ........................ 189

**F.** PARTING WITH ADAPA - Edouard d'Araille .................... 201

"BEFORE
UTNAPISHTIM WAS HUMAN –
BUT NOW LET
UTNAPISHTIM AND HIS WIFE
BECOME
JUST LIKE US GODS

AND HE
SHALL
DWELL
FAR AWAY
AT THE SOURCE
OF THE RIVERS"

# PUBLISHER'S NOTE

'ADAPA'S ASCENT' is <u>Volume Number 1</u> in the new *Great World Books*™ collection from LIVING TIME BOOKS - and for this reason alone it deserves a few special words of introduction. One key purpose of the *Great World Books*™ series is to publish neglected works of great literature - books that have been forgotten about, texts that have been overlooked, as well as authors who have only recently been discovered.

In the case of *Adapa's Ascent*, there is a combination of these factors. On the one hand it is true that for a period of as long as one and a half millennia, this work was passed down in written form and appreciated as a classic — yet sadly, with the decimation of the Babylonian Empire, this and many other vital works were lost for over two thousand years.

However, with the fortuitous discovery of tens of thousands of cuneiform tablets in the 19th Century, key works of Mesopotamian literature resurfaced, though it has taken a very long time to decipher them and work out exactly what has been recovered.

For some years now, the legend of 'Adapa' has been a prized and much appreciated Akkadian text in the scholarly community. However, in spite of a great deal of academic attention, it is almost wholly unknown to the wider reading public. For them, the only work of Mesopotamian literature that exists is the first epic, that of 'Gilgamesh'. The current obsession with world records and winners so often means that if something is in second place - not the superlative in a particular category - then it is likely to be ignored and left to one side, and to an unjust extent.

It is possible that 'Gilgamesh' has received the lion's share of notice by readers because it is a story replete with action, love and danger to a degree that is easily appreciated by a modern audience. The tale of Adapa, however - even though far shorter and not filled with as many exciting plot-points as its bigger brother - is a truly significant narrative that can be approached from many different angles and is certainly not lacking in high drama or real intrigue.

Now, hopefully, *this* volume will give 'Adapa' an opportunity to redress the misbalance of attention and draw a new generation of readers into discovering this very different piece of Mesopotamian fiction that has, up to this point, never been published as a complete work of literature in a poetic format.

At least not since the days of Babylon.

The project of bringing *Adapa's Ascent* into print as a work of world literature has been one that was planned by LIVING TIME BOOKS for many years — it is only regrettable that it has taken such a long time to come to fruition. Nonetheless, it is hoped that this end result will be worth the wait and that such an ancient work - though in a fresh form - will succeed in reaching a new public in search of old literature.

Concerning the substance of this book, at the core of this volume is Edouard d'Araille's English verse translation of the cuneiform tablets that tell the story of the mythical Adapa. This translation has been based on sources from three different periods, from the 18th Century BCE to the 7th Century BCE.

Numerous additional materials are provided in this book. It is our hope that they will make the work more accessible and understandable to readers.

This verse translation is preceded by the essay 'The Birth of Fiction', which explores the beginnings of world literature and how the legend of Adapa figures within that. It also includes some reflection on the work's contents and perspectives on its meaning.

Several other extra materials are furnished after the text of the poem which may also be helpful in comprehending and interpreting that work. There is a 'Character Glossary' that gives some basic knowledge about the central players within *Adapa's Ascent* and a critical essay - subtitled 'Recreating an Ancient Classic' - that describes in some detail how this poetic translation has been pieced together from fragments.

Images of the original sources are provided in one of the appendices (photographs of all the tablets on which the text is based) and Edouard d'Araille also provides a 'Translation Sketch' of the earliest known version of the Adapa narrative which was written in Sumerian (circa 18th Century BCE). Also of value to those who wish to research *Adapa's Ascent* further, some 'Suggestions for Further Reading' are provided so as to guide deeper research into the text.

Alderson Smith - SERIES EDITOR
GREAT WORLD BOOKS ™

# ACKNOWLEDGEMENTS

There are too many people to thank for me to possibly mention them all here. The scholars in Assyriology who are included in the bibliography - as well as so many more I did not have the space to include - are owed my unrepayable debt of thanks for the many works of theirs to which I referred throughout the composition of this translation. Some - such as Professor Thorkild Jacobsen and Nancy K. Sandars - I discovered decades ago, while others - like Professors Shlomo Izre'el, Antoine Cavigneaux and Andrew George - I became aware of only more recently. To all those experts I also owe my deepest apologies for all of the ways in which I may have misunderstood or misinterpreted their articles, monographs and translations. It is my hope that, in spite of the errors that I have certainly committed, there will nonetheless be some elements of value in the volume that I present here. I am an *amateur* of this subject in the most literal way possible: I fell in love with Mesopotamia a long time ago and I have never ceased to be excited and stimulated by all that I learn about this most primal of civilizations with its spectacular culture and achievements. — I have been rewarded immensely by perusing the rich harvest of literature produced by Assyriologists over the last century and a half, but I must openly acknowledge that what I have written is a work of poetry and not a product of pure scholarship. I have never found a book more difficult to write, but it is to the 'Sumero-Akkadians' that this book owes its existence. I also give special thanks to the British Library - where I undertook much of my research - and the British Museum, where some of the invaluable Adapa tablets currently reside.

*Edouard d'Araille*                                    *January 2020*

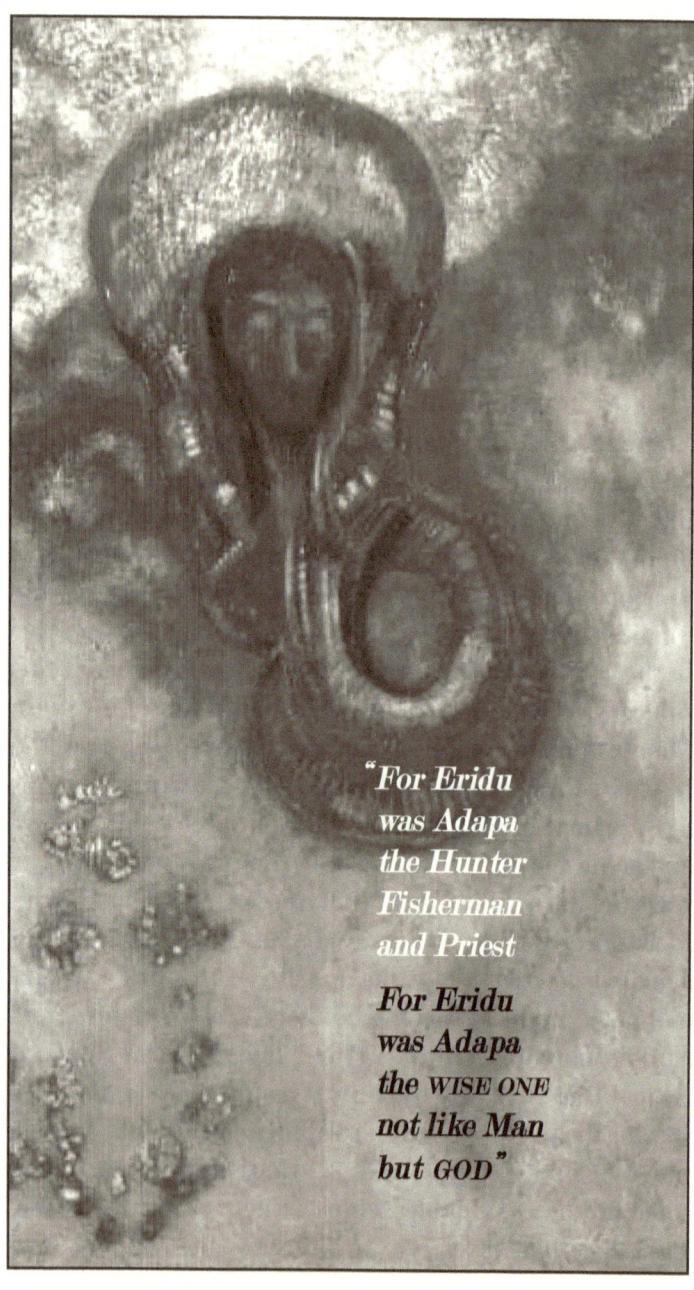

*"For Eridu
was Adapa
the Hunter
Fisherman
and Priest*

**For Eridu
was Adapa
the WISE ONE
not like Man
but GOD"**

# THE BIRTH OF FICTION
### *by* Edouard d'Araille

"WHERE WILL FICTION END?" is a question that it is near impossible to answer. - *"When did Fiction begin?"* on the other hand, is a question to which we may find *some answers*, although perhaps not any definitive or final ones at this very moment in time.

## I. IN THE BEGINNING

*"In the Beginning was the Word"*
**GOSPEL OF JOHN 1:1**

I WASN'T MUCH INTERESTED in Ancient Culture as a kid. Sure, I was scared to death by Boris Karloff portraying 'The Mummy' - and totally captivated by Mr. Clayton (my only First Grade teacher who knew how to kill off boredom) when he told us about the 'Pyramid Power' that was capable of *recharging batteries, resharpening blades*, even *magnetizing wealth!* - As for the Greeks, all that I knew of was Homer (not Simpson) and Hercules' Tasks - though I had not an inkling what they were. Of the Romans? Just that they built damn straight roads and regurgitated their food at endless series of banquets - *how gross!*
          I was stunned to discover, at about 20 years of age, that there was *another ancient culture* that had outstripped all others in every arena of progress and civilization - that of the Mesopotamians. I would go

on to learn that this people - living from about 5500 to 550 BCE - discovered literally dozens of vital inventions before anyone else and that they made progress in virtually every area of human enterprise to a degree that had not been achieved by any societies existing before. In fact, I learnt that they have a genuine claim to being the *first civilization* to appear on Earth.

The earliest of the Mesopotamian people were called the 'Sumerians' and it was in the 5th Millennium BCE that they developed agriculture; by the 4th Millennium BCE they had mastered the arts; by the 3rd Millennium BCE they had invented writing (thus written history began). - We will return to that accomplishment later to consider it in more detail.

In a region that now occupies most of Iraq, Kuwait, some parts of Northern Saudi Arabia, eastern parts of Syria, South-Eastern Turkey and some stretches on the Turkish-Syrian and Iran-Iraq borders — within this region, first known by the name *Mesopotamia*, human culture was truly to flourish. Geographically, it was based around the river systems of the Tigris and Euphrates - the actual name 'Mesopotamia' meaning "between the two rivers".

Even after a cursory survey of their achievements, I was dumbfounded by the sheer quantity and significance of their contributions to man's advancement. I found it hard to believe that I had been taught nothing about them at school - especially considering that the earliest inhabitants of Mesopotamia, the

Sumerians, had been the ones who pioneered all of the subjects I studied (or failed to) at college: mathematics, politics, literature, law, technology and so many more. There is barely an area of human invention in which the first Mesopotamians did not excel.

They invented the wheel (and along with that the chariot), created the very first sailing (and fishing) boats, built impressive, highly functional works of architecture — plus the mastery of farming (and therefore food production) is something that we owe to them more than any other civilization. Foremost within that last area of innovation, the Sumerians invented the plough and the first agricultural irrigation systems - which latter addition made it possible for them to produce a variety of crops in areas that would otherwise have stayed arid and unproductive.

The Sumerians drew up the earliest maps, began to record astronomical observations, devised the 24-hour time system - with the earliest 'clocks' being candles marked off into twenty-four segments, thus showing how much time had passed - and were even the originators of the division of hours into sixty minutes (and minutes into sixty seconds). The reason for this was that this ancient people did not have a metric system of counting like us - where '10' is the primary basis of mathematics - but a 'sexagesimal' system: one in which division into '60s' is at the core of how most arithmetical calculations are made.

As concerns their methods of temporal measurement, it is interesting to note - in passing - that the Mesopotamian minute in fact lasted four times as long as a modern minute! However this may be, the Sumerians not only gave us the smaller division of hours into minutes, but they divided their days and nights into two series of twelve hours - as their number system was also 'duodecimal' (based upon number 12).

That, however, is as much time as we have to discuss the *general* innovativeness of the Sumerians. The invention that is really behind the appearance of this book is probably their most important creation of all - one that would impact the history and growth of civilizations from their period onwards.

The most significant discovery of the Sumerians was that of *writing* itself - without which you would not be reading these words at all. Their language was the earliest to be inscribed in a form that could be read by others. The method of writing that the earliest Mesopotamians developed, is described as 'Cuneiform' (meaning 'wedge-shaped'), because the symbols set down were created with the wedge-shaped markings of a blunt reed upon a soft clay tablet. Clay would then dry out, sometimes assisted in doing so by being baked by the sun, and these tablets were kept in personal and public libraries in a similar way to how modern repositories house books and periodicals.

Originally, cuneiform writing looked much like *pictograms* - picture symbols, akin to the hieroglyphics of the Egyptians - but over time these developed into an alphabet of letters that would prove to be the precursor of most western alphabets that came later. The Mesopotamian languages would develop from the Sumerian into the Akkadian, through the Assyrian into the Babylonian, and eventually - by the First Millennium BCE - cuneiform inscriptions would become extinct and be replaced by the 22-consonant Phoenician alphabet. From this was derived the Greek alphabet and from that in turn the Latin. The rest, as they say, is history - for those two languages would go on to reign supreme for almost two thousand years as two of the most important channels for the transmission and exchange of knowledge.

Returning to the start of the story of writing, it was at the beginning of the 4th Millennium BCE that the ancient Sumerians began to record their monetary transactions in an early form of cuneiform script. I don't think it is surprising that financial documents - such as accounts, receipts, wage-slips, invoices, wills *etc.* - appear to be the initial examples of recorded writing, as the fiscal side of life had developed into a more quantifiable form than ever before with the invention of the first forms of money itself. Trading had become more than just barter and therefore it is little wonder that, with monetary transactions taking place, it was necessary to devise ways of recording the exchange of currencies and merchandise.

By roughly 2600 BCE, the Sumerian form of cuneiform writing had evolved to the point that its symbols actually represented syllables of the spoken language. Therefore, from this point in time onwards we find transcriptions of poems, songs and prayers. Lullabies, for instance, are one of the earliest examples of lyrics being recorded - dating back almost five thousand years - probably because the ancient Sumerians needed reliable ways of calming babies to sleep just as much as we do now! Whereas a parent today will turn to 'Youtube' in order to find a video to accomplish this purpose, five millennia ago cuneiform writing did an admirable job of recording the sleep songs for babies in a format that could be handed down from one generation of parents to the next.

The early Mesopotamians made use of their invention of writing in many of the ways that we continue to use it still: they recorded their laws and regulations; they saw to it that delicious recipes were shared and not forgotten; they wrote letters to each other - and even the first type of 'Royal Mail' came into existence as high dignitaries used the earliest forms of correspondence to exchange holy and royal decrees that needed transmitting between religious leaders and government. They also used writing to record ideas and proverbs - even riddles and jokes. Whatever you can think of using writing for nowadays — chances are the Sumerians did so as well.

In some ways - working with the little that we know in terms of dating the cuneiform documents that have survived - there appears to be a natural order in which writing progressed. We begin with the recording of *monetary concerns* (transactions, contracts, wills), then move to the transcription of key documents concerning the *functioning of family, state and religion* (lullabies, recipes, laws, letters, rites and prayers), while the setting down of *literature* (poetry, myths, epics *etc.*) comes later still than the recording of their financial and practical matters. — This is not to say that no evidence exists of myths, poetry and fiction earlier on, but from the limited library of tablets that have been discovered up to now, there does seem to be a gradual pattern of the development of writings, from the pragmatic to the intellectual, so that as we move forwards in time there is a greater quantity of literary and artistic texts being produced.

In the mid-nineteenth century, a fourteen year-old school drop-out living in England - by the name of *George Smith* - was working as an engraver of banknotes in London. At lunchtimes, however, this curious youth spent the bulk of his time browsing through the voluminous holdings of the British Museum, and after some years - in 1866 - the staff of this venerable institution noticed him at last. He became employed as an assistant in the cataloguing and analysis of the tens of thousands of cuneiform tablets (so many of them fragmentary) that had been shipped there years ago and been stuck in storage — neglected and unexplored. He set himself to the task with passion, studying these archives for over ten years solid.

From the mid-19th Century onwards, excavations in Mesopotamia had yielded some of the oldest written texts known to man: twenty-five thousand tablets had been sent back to the British Museum - lingering there in complete obscurity for years. Few people were capable of even beginning to decipher the cuneiform tablets. The texts remained a conundrum that only the rarest of scholars could hope to solve. Young Mr. Smith, however, had learned much from the elite within this field - Austen Henry Layard, Henry Rawlinson, Hormuzd Rassam - and he managed to translate texts that had never been decoded before.

One day, quite out of the blue, George Smith lets rip a roar of delight, leaps out of his chair and tears his shirt off, commencing to run around the room like someone gone mad. It turns out that he had just discovered a passage about a 'Great Flood', which appeared to give independent corroboration to the deluge that Noah experiences in Genesis. In the passage that George Smith translated, all of humanity dies and only one man - known as Utnapishtim - survives that flood. When, in 1872, he reported his findings to the 'Society for Biblical Archaeology', it became front-page news across the papers of Europe. Prime ministers, royalty, intellectuals and the general public attended talks on the historic nature of his finds — it was as *big* as the Tomb of Tutankhamun!

What George Smith had uncovered would eventually become Tablet 11 of the 'Gilgamesh' epic: generally considered to be the oldest story ever written. Over the two decades that followed, the rest of its narrative was pieced together from a number of separate tablets and it turned out that the earliest versions of the text dated back as far as 2150 BCE.

It was actually in 1849 that the first discovery of library ruins from the reign of the 7th Century BCE Assyrian King Ashurbanipal occurred. Altogether, around 30,000 documents from his Royal Library were found, though a great many of them were fragments. It was among these literary remains that the most complete form of the epic of Gilgamesh was found.

Ashurbanipal had as his aim to assemble a library to rival all other libraries then in existence, therefore the discovery of works inside this library indicates to some extent the value that was, at that time, placed on the documents that were housed within its collections. Not only was the 'Gilgamesh' epic featured there but also a narrative work called 'Adapa', which is the focus of this volume. Few archaeological finds have been as significant and invaluable as that of the Library of King Ashurbanipal. Indeed, H.G. Wells comments in his 'Outline of History' that it is: *"the most precious source of historical material in the world"* — barely an exaggeration. The contents of this library caused truly seismic changes in the evolution of our knowledge of Mesopotamia.

'Gilgamesh' has since become one of the true classics of world literature, not simply because of its great ancestry, but to a large extent due to the sheer power and vibrancy of its storytelling. Based in part on the life of a real King Gilgamesh (who lived some time between 2800-2500 BCE in the town of Uruk and was revered as a God after his death), that epic tells the story of his friendship with Enkidu, their battle with the beast Humbaba and - ultimately - Gilgamesh's loss of his best friend and subsequent quest for the secret of immortality. In the end, however, he is unable to hold onto the secret that he discovers.

As for the myth of Adapa, although what is now known as 'Fragment D' had been published by George Smith in his 'Chaldean Account of the Genesis' (pp.125-126) in 1876, he had no idea that it was part of that story. Indeed, on p.306 of that same publication he expressed his surprise that: "*the legend of Oannes* [Adapa], *which must have been one of the Babylonian stories of the Creation, has not yet been discovered*". Mr. Smith believed that the fragment he had discovered was a part of the 'Erra' narrative, and it was only after the publication of a more complete version of the Adapa narrative - called the 'Amarna Tablet' - that Assyriological scholar Archibald Sayce identified that they were both part of the same plot.

There are numerous other fiction works from Mesopotamia, but for the sake of focus - and because they have several themes in common - we shall limit our discussions to 'Gilgamesh' and 'Adapa' alone. Epic fragments about legendary King Enmerkar (credited with the invention of writing), Lugulbanda (who may have been his successor), Inanna (known as 'Queen of Heaven' and 'Goddess of Love') and, most famously, tales writing of the *World's Creation* and *Great Flood* - all these also merit the attention of those wishing to appreciate this early era of fiction.

## II. STORYTELLING

*"I tell you a story so as
to tell you who I am"*

WHAT DISTINGUISHES Humans from Animals?
- this is a question that has been posed ever since the
beginning of speculative thought and it has been answered so many different ways that it would not be
possible to document them all here if one wanted to.
Some say that the ability to create fire is what distinguishes humans from beasts, others that 'reason'
is the especially human faculty that divides us from
the animals - then again there are those who point
to man's two-legged status as a determining feature,
or that humans possess 'self-consciousness' while all
of the "lesser species" do not. I am not going to make
any comments on the proposed distinguishing characteristics above. Each of them has some truth in it but
none of them strikes me as being the special feature
that sets humans apart from animals most distinctly.

In my opinion - *and that is all it is* - there is
nothing that identifies the human being more absolutely than their capacity *to relate stories to each
other*. Language, numerous professors will argue, is
the unique possession of mankind - and it is hard to
argue with that - but even if animals were able to
speak (as some believe the dolphins do, in their own
ultrasonic language), I sincerely doubt that they
would display this special tendency that we have to

tell stories to each other. In my view, words are the fuel of mankind's intelligence and stories are the fires that burn when we express our experiences in a narrative fashion, telling our tales to one another.

It is twenty years ago that I listened to a Belgian professor of linguistics, called Pierre Van Den Heuvel, giving a talk on the nature of narrative in the works of one modern French author. His words, which still resonate with me from then, are those with which I have opened this section of the essay. In fact, they were a *slight variation* of those on the preceding page, the exact words being: "*When I tell you a story, I tell you who I am*". This seems to me to convey a fundamental truth about storytelling — that it is not about recording something objective and absolute, but about each one of us (who tells a story) sharing something personal with those to whom we relate our stories. In telling you a story, I actually let you into my world, my personal life, and tell you something of significance *about who I really am.*

In the previous section, we have considered how the earliest Mesopotamians - the Sumerians - were in all likelihood the originators of written fiction. This is not to say that it is impossible that fiction was not written earlier, elsewhere - for future archaeological finds may provide evidence of fiction recorded in writing from other, more ancient civilizations. Perhaps we are yet to discover a *bona fide* story from Egypt, or even China, that predates 'Gilgamesh' and wins the contest of temporal priority. We will never be able to ascertain the moment that the first tale was told, in the same way that we will never be able to know when and where words were first uttered. In my opinion, the question of precisely *who* wrote the mother of all stories is of far less importance than *why* that story was initially written - or why we feel it is important to tell stories to each other *per se*. For that reason, I wish to reflect on this for a brief moment before we return to take a preliminary look at the story which is the central focus of this volume.

Though it is so natural to consider the emergence of language as a key factor that made possible the communication of stories between people, words are by no means the necessary prerequisite to telling a story. When you consider that comic strips (even with no captions or speech bubbles) can convey stories in an effective manner, it is not possible to rule out that the earliest cave paintings - and other forms of primitive art - were attempts by our predecessors to share stories among themselves. The old proverb that, "*A picture is worth a thousand words*," has some truth to it, and before words were even invented it is possible that the pictures of scenes that we find - for example, in the caves of Lascaux - were narrative accounts, in a graphic form, that represented personal stories being shared between the members of a group.

Moving forwards thousands of years in time, what else is the 'Bayeux Tapestry', dating back to the

Eleventh Century, than a 70-meter long embroidered cloth providing a '*story in pictures*' of the key events leading up to the Norman conquest of England, culminating in the famous Battle of Hastings. There is no question that pictures have been considered to be a truly effective way in which to tell stories — and I emphasize this point because I do not believe storytelling began with the ability of our species to tell each other stories *with words*, but with our ability to relate stories to each other *in any manner whatsoever*, pictures being only one way in which to do so.

I think that it is also noteworthy that the first alphabets and words themselves derive from 'pictograms' or 'pictographs' - meaning pictorial symbols which partially resemble what they signify. A symbol for a 'person', for example, could look like an elementary diagram of a person, the symbol for a 'tree' might be a simple icon of a tree, and so forth. Looking at the language of the ancient Egyptians, their written vocabulary is composed of hieroglyphics and not words in the modern sense. For this reason, although there do exist Egyptian stories written as early as those of the Sumerians, the latter have been granted precedence in terms of storywriting because their narrative literature was *written using words* and not pictorial symbols. In reality, the first forms of Sumerian writing were themselves pictographs (or 'picture words'), the signs closely resembling the objects they represented - grain, bread, head *etc.* - and were an immediate precursor to cuneiform words.

On a fundamental level, language has for a long time been seen as the key ability that separates humans from animals, a view accepted by the Mesopotamian. Homo *Sapiens* are '*knowing* beings', whereas other creatures only experience life - they do not think about it. While animals only perceive the world outside them, *we* are able to conceive of a world inside our minds. With *concepts* in our heads for every thing that we experience in our lives, we simultaneously possess *words* to communicate about those thought-forms. Whereas a dog only chews on the bone, I am able to think of 'the bone' and visualize it in my mind's eye — and if I want someone else to think about that, it is enough if I use the word which is an index for that concept.

What freedom this gives us is incredible, for it means that we are not limited by the world that is outside us but we are able to handle a world in our 'imagination' - the name we have given to this incredible theatre of possibilities. *There* we are not tied down to the real and actual. We can describe not only *what has happened to us* - with many variations of style and content - but also represent events that have never happened to us: those which perhaps *we wish to have happened*. In fact, so far as the arena of the imagination is concerned, there are no limits to what we can think of and describe. For this reason, humans are liberated from their immediate situation in a way that animals never can be. Storytelling provides us with the near-magical ability to create things and events that have 'reality' perhaps only in our minds.

What I think is so special about this ability to tell a story, is that even in the simplest instance of storytelling, where I - the storyteller - relate a story about something that has in point of fact happened to me, the story allows me to convey a series of events even though they are no longer occurring. Being situated at a later moment in time than that which I am talking about, even if I use the first person ('I') in order to tell my story, I am still at one remove of reality from the 'happening-time' of the events that I am relating. When I tell you, "*I walked over the bridge and found myself at the edge of a green and fertile field*", it conjures up a picture of these events, as if they were happening all over again. In fact, by using the present tense to relate this story it can be made to feel more 'present' to those being told the story. It is worth reflecting that in several languages - especially those at a more primitive stage in their development - the same verb-forms are used for the past, present and future tenses, the difference in time being appreciated through context and not grammar.

Taking it one stage further though, once the storyteller speaks of him- or her-self as if they were another person, and refers to their self by name and with the word 'he' or 'she' (where previously they had used the personal pronoun 'I') — once this happens, the account both becomes more distant from the reality that they had originally experienced *and more real as a story in itself*. Once I tell you that, "*Nathaniel walked over the bridge and found himself at the edge of a green and fertile field*", it sounds like something different from mere memory. The words appear to convey a world of the past or of the imagination, in a way that they did not before. The storyteller, with the power of their words, is able to make up anything that they please and make us believe that what it is recounting is 'real' - in such a way that *it matters to us*.

When we read stories from previous generations, even from extinct civilizations (like Mesopotamia), I think that it is easy to forget what the stories *meant* to the people among whom they originated. To us - mere outsiders from a distant time - we are too liable to approach the fiction that we read as just another artifact from the past and not as what was once a *living reality* (albeit in the form of fiction) for the audiences who existed then. I believe that stories were told, not just as a mere pastime - which can sometimes be the case, that is true - but *because they needed to be told*. When I think about the tales that were being shared in Sumeria (two of which we are about to look at in more detail), I cannot help but reflect that these stories represented, not just new stories, but the emergence of a whole new area of writing in itself — that of fiction storytelling. Thinking about this, I am tempted to believe that there must have been immensely important reasons why this entirely new species of writing was born. In terms of what a seminal achievement *fiction* would prove itself to be, it seems to me to be equivalent - in the area of literature - to what the invention of the wheel was in the domain of transportation. With fiction, writing becomes completely freed from reality, though I do not believe that the Sumerians considered their stories to be merely *fictitious* at the time they were producing them; nor do I think that the Greeks - a thousand years later - looked upon Homer's creations as *just fiction*. They possessed a serious *reality* for their audiences.

The problem is that, after four thousand years of storytelling - and our realization that stories are not real but fabrications - to say that something is "just fiction" has become a derogatory term, too close to saying that something is "nothing but lies". However, when the early inhabitants of Mesopotamia came up with Gods and 'Ultra-Mortals' - possessing superpowers that could vie with the Gods - I do not believe they considered their stories as being in any way 'made up' or merely imaginary. I believe that these people were convinced they were providing a *real narrative* of Humans and Gods, one that explained the workings of their Cosmos and everything happening in it.

When we read stories by the Sumerians, we are given a glimpse of what this people really believed - *and were*. Returning to the quote with which this chapter opened, when these early Mesopotamians tell us a story, *they tell us who they were*. This is why stories are so vital — for through them the inhabitants of one civilization can tell us "what made them tick", and we (living thousands of years distant from them) can appreciate their essence. Stories communicate the nature of *their* Humanity. Stories make *us* Human.

## III. FIRST STORY

*"Most people, in fact, will not take
the trouble in finding out the truth
- but are much more inclined to
accept the first story they hear."*
THUCYDIDES

HAVING ENTITLED THIS SECTION 'First Story', I feel the onus is on me to explain why I would be so bold as to suggest this about 'Adapa'. It is widely accepted that the 'Epic of Gilgamesh' is the first surviving work of literature, existing in its earliest form as a cycle of five poems from the Third Dynasty of Ur in Sumeria - and dating back to around 2100 BCE. However, even though 'Gilgamesh' may indeed be the first written work of literature, this does not mean that we will not still discover an older work of literature in the future, nor that stories were not *told* earlier.

In fact, finding a single definitive answer to the question, *"What were the first stories ever told?"* is absolutely impossible - yet that does not mean that we cannot speculate about what these stories may have been by referring to the earliest stories of which we have a record in writing, as well as paying attention to those stories which have only been set down in a pictorial form? It would be amazing to make a full survey of the oldest stories existing from cultures as diverse as Egypt, China, India, New Zealand and Native American Indians — from the 'Pyramid Texts' to the 'Rig Veda' — though that would require a whole volume to itself and contributions from the world's leading scholars on these widely ranging cultures.

What I wish to focus on in this section are my personal reasons for considering the story of 'Adapa' to have a just claim to being the *first story*. This is not to say that it is the story of which we currently possess the first historical copy - nor that I have the *unobtainable knowledge* that this was the first story ever told between human beings. I do not assert this is proven in any way, though I do believe that *Adapa's* tale is perhaps the most significant of the earliest stories. I have a number of observations to make which dovetail together in supporting the tentative view that 'Adapa' is, in a significant way, the *First Story*. However, I do not want it to be misunderstood that I am suggesting this piece of literature "beats Gilgamesh" in a way that cannot be shown with documentary evidence at this point in time - so let me explain.

Until recently, the key tablets that had been discovered - documenting the story of Adapa - dated back between approximately 1400 BCE and 700 BCE. It was the earliest tablets of 'Adapa' - in Akkadian cuneiform - which contained the most complete telling of the Adapa narrative. However, in the early 1980's a great find of Sumerian texts was made near Tell Haddad (in modern-day Iraq) and this included two earlier Sumerian versions of the Adapa story, dating back to approximately 1760 BCE — therefore roughly four centuries older than any versions previously known.

This was an amazing step forward in a realization that the story of Adapa might go back further in time than ever suspected. However, deeper investigations reveal that there are references to the character of Adapa *further back in time still.* For example, there are rituals from Nippur dating back to 1800 BCE which use Adapa's name in their incantations, and the 19th century BCE text 'The Chronicle of Esagila' clearly mentions Adapa in one line of text, where it says: "*The sage Adapa, son of* ", before it breaks off without us knowing the end of the line. However, it is likely - if later texts give us any clue - that the complete line might have been: "*The sage Adapa, son of Enki* ". However, due to the brief nature of this reference to Adapa, it is apparent that Adapa was a figure who did not need much mention — that he was by that time an accepted part of the cultural history of the Mesopotamians then thriving.

Although it can be disputed, there are a few places in stories of as early a date as 'Enmerkar and the Lord of Aratta' (21st Century BCE) where incomplete reference appears to be made to 'The Sage' (potentially Adapa) and it needs to be seen whether new excavations - or references discovered within texts that are still being deciphered - will uncover verifications of the myth of Adapa existing at this time, or even earlier. What would be most significant, would be to find evidence of the myth of Adapa earlier than the 21st century BCE — *before* that period from which we have the first poems on 'Gilgamesh'.

What we are not able to determine though, is how early 'Adapa' was being circulated as a myth and how this story came into being - whether it was based on an actual living person (as Gilgamesh appears to have been) or whether he was only a fictitious character. What 'Gilgamesh' and 'Adapa' do appear to have in common is that they had both been expressed in a mature form between 1400-1300 BCE and each had reached a standardized form (that would continue to be handed down) by the 7th Century BCE.

When one looks at these two stories alongside each other, even though there is a superficial similarity of theme - in terms of 'Immortality' - the nature of their writing is so different that they seem to belong to two different classes of fiction altogether. While 'Gilgamesh' poems tell us the story of its hero with numerous episodes and sequences of adventure and emotion, 'Adapa' is sparse in events and simple in its form, not taking us on any substantial journey in its short narrative. However, the story it tells us is one of significance - one that seems to have served several explanatory functions for those who knew it.

'Adapa', so much less developed in its literary form than 'Gilgamesh' - in terms of narrative techniques, writing style and fictional adventurousness - appears like the younger of two brothers to me. In fact, it is even as if one work were more like a parent, the other a child, so much more primal is the story of 'Adapa' compared with that of 'Gilgamesh'. Viewed alongside each other, the plot of 'Adapa' seems quite infantile in comparison with the complexity of the 'Gilgamesh' drama. One relevant comparison that can be found with the storyline of 'Adapa' - both in terms of its simplicity and narrative structure - is the famous story of 'Adam and Eve' in the book of Genesis.

The difference is that the first recensions of 'Adapa' date back around one thousand years before the first appearance of Adam and Eve in the bible. It is quite possible that the authors of the texts that compose 'Genesis' were aware of the story of 'Adapa', and when you look at the names of these two central characters, they certainly bear a superficial resemblance to each other. Whereas 'Adapa' is derived from a Sumerian word meaning 'Wise', and Adapa (also known as 'Oannes') comes from the water - which makes sense, as his father is the 'Lord of the Deep', Enki - the name 'Adam' means 'Man', or more completely 'Man born of Earth'. Each of them is presented as an elemental man, who occupies a position of being the forefather of all the peoples who come afterwards. Each of them is *primordial*, for the story of their existence is used to explain the existence of other human beings. Also, each of them is warned against partaking of something dangerous.

However, even though the 'Adapa' story is of much earlier origin than that of 'Adam', Adapa is a man who appears *after* a great flood and is one of several humans who cooperate with the Gods in order to establish life on earth — while Adam, at least in the sequence of the Bible stories, comes *before* the flood story that we read of featuring Noah (in the book of Genesis too). The earliest version of 'Adapa' is perhaps the most fascinating, for we are provided with a series of events which occurs before the establishment of civilization on earth (*qv*. Appendix 4 - 'Translation Sketch'). Just like Adam is presented as the 'First Man' in the bible story, Adapa is presented as the Proto-Human whose life and example all others follow. It is not that Adapa exists before all other men and women - which is how Adam is represented in the Old Testament - but because *he forms a crucial link between the Gods and Men*, like the many Greek Gods who came later, a 'Son of God' like Adam also.

Though Adapa does appear as a unique character in Mesopotamian mythology, there are close similarities between him and some other key figures we discover in their stories. For example, the person of 'Atrahasis' (whose name means 'most wise') is presented as a man who has survived a great flood and - like Adapa - established life for humanity on earth. 'The Epic of Atrahasis' - which includes preservation of male and female animals on an 'Ark', like in the story of Noah - dates back to a century later than the first full versions of 'Adapa, though the stories of a Great Flood date back even further than 2300 BCE.

My own opinion is that further investigation of the similarities between *Adapa* and *Atrahasis* may bear fruit, though at the moment these characters are seen as wholly distinct from one another. Most scholars agree that Utnapishtim (*qv*. 'Gilgamesh') and Ziusudra

- also presented as being the named heroes who survive a 'Great Flood', and (in some versions) as having attained the secret of Immortality - *are the same as* 'Atrahasis'. Perhaps, once the analysis of Mesopotamian history has matured through further centuries of scholarship, we will know a greater amount about the interconnection of these diluvian heroes, who bear striking similarities.

Returning to 'Adapa' — whether or not there exist versions of this story that predate 'Gilgamesh', it is clear from texts that we do possess, that Adapa is considered to be a primal character who has emerged after a cataclysmic flood and established order on Earth through wisdom and resourcefulness. From the texts of 'Adapa' that survive, we learn that he is skillful in many areas (fishing, hunting, crafts), has wide knowledge of the world, is a religious leader and man of law - even the source of man's abilities to cure all human illness. In artwork, as well as in written texts, Adapa is represented as being more than human, as a half-fish/half-man figure who, by day, comes to the shore of the Persian Gulf and teaches mankind all about writing, arts, sciences and knowledge in general, having been sent to humankind by his father Ea (or Enki) - the God of the Waters and of Wisdom.

Ultimately, though, the story of Adapa does more than provide us with a 'First Story' - insofar as it tells us the account of a progenitor of civilization - for 'Adapa' also provides its audience with an explanation of *what distinguishes Gods and Men from each other* on the most fundamental level. Although the Mesopotamians *did* see language as a defining distinction between man and animals - between man and Gods there was an additional defining feature whose origins the story of Adapa tried to elucidate:

*Man is mortal* and *Gods are immortal* - those are, more than anything else, the key truths at the core of the 'Adapa' texts. By showing us how Adapa rejected the gifts of *Immortal Life* in Heaven, the authors of this story have given a reason why **man** (who is represented by Adapa, as the prototypical human) **is mortal** and therefore consigned to living on earth. Gods are, by nature immortal, and reside in Heaven. We shall look at the actual plot of that story in Section IV, where there will be time to look at this dichotomy between humanity and the Gods further.

It has not been my aim to arrive at any earth-shattering conclusions about the 'Adapa' story in this introduction, only to share with you a few thoughts and opinions that have crossed my mind in the course of spending time with the texts of 'Adapa'.

The way that the character of Adapa has been referred to by name in texts *over four thousand years old*, it seems - to my mind - that he was a personage whose history is so accepted and established in the minds of the Mesopotamians that it was not necessary to do any more than refer to him in passing for the readers (or audience) to be reminded of his story. Just as a text might make passing reference to Adam or Jesus, Napoleon or Hitler (as two more notorious examples) without having to recount detailed histories so as to bring to mind archetypal stories before the public's consciousness - I believe that it was superfluous for a writer at the start of the 2nd Millennium BCE to make any more than a simple nod to 'Adapa' in order to call to mind his narrative to the public. His was a story that was possibly known to everyone.

How far back the origins of this vital Sumerian icon stretch, it is very difficult to say. Whether texts will emerge that show that the story of 'Adapa' predates even the first versions of 'Gilgamesh' — that is impossible to say until new excavations prove or disprove that possibility. What I feel certain of, is that already by the close of the 3rd Millennium BCE, Adapa's story was one that was widely known by the people of Sumer and that it was used in order to explain both the relations between Gods and mankind, as also the way in which *civilization* had been established on Earth - which history tells us occurred in that region at an earlier date and in a maturer form than anywhere else on our planet. So much we know.

When I refer to 'Adapa's Ascent' with the subtitle "*The First Story*", I do so both because I am personally convinced that it *may* predate Gilgamesh in its appearance as a story and because - due to the substance of its narrative - it is a story that aims to tell us the *origins* of the distinction between Gods and Man. Its aim is to tell us the 'First Story' - one at whose heart we find the persona of *Adapa*, the 'First Man'.

## INTERLUDE - A Tale
## of Two Brothers

AS 'GILGAMESH' HAS ENTERED our discussion of 'Adapa' so substantially already, I would like to take a moment to consider these two works of fiction alongside each other, before focusing our attention almost exclusively on the latter work for the remainder of this introduction. I would like to take a look at what makes these two works so different from each other, in spite of their possessing at least one theme in common: that of man's concern with *Immortality*.

However, even though these two stories seem to share a theme of 'Immortal Life', I think that it may be a superficial similarity. For while in the case of Gilgamesh, immortality becomes an element of his quest - and he goes to great lengths to discover the secret from Utnapishtim towards the end of that epic - in 'Adapa', immortality is something that the main character has *at no point been actively seeking* and he is tricked out of accepting it without even realizing what he has accidentally rejected! - But more on this in a moment, once we survey its plot as a whole.

When I read 'Gilgamesh', its main character is presented as being "two parts God and one part Man" — he comes across as a larger than life personality, yet one who is at the same time earthly and real in how he is described. If historical records are to be believed, Gilgamesh was an actual king in early Sumeria, one who was later to be recognized as a God. What strikes me most about how he is depicted in the epic poems through which he has been immortalized, is how very *humanly* he is described. In 'Gilgamesh', one does not meet the refined hero with high and worthy values - instead one comes face to face with a brutish womanizer whose, "*lust leaves no virgin to her lover, neither the warrior's daughter nor the wife of the noble*". The whole work - though modern editions have been synthesized from several sources and some may not exactly represent any version that existed in Mesopotamia - is written in a punchy, fast-moving and thrilling way that makes it appear to me like a popular entertainment of its day. Like a Hollywood movie, it has action, romance, fight sequences, suspense and great twists. In fact, the authors of the time (however many there were) have pulled out all the stops to make 'Gilgamesh' into an exciting, suspenseful adventure tale with something for everyone. When you cut to the chase, 'Gilgamesh' has more in common with 'buddy movie' than high epic - Enkidu and Gilgamesh, the bromance's heroes, beating the fearful and mighty foe Humbaba, as a duo; only at that point, this unpredictable yarn turns into something more like a dark arthouse movie, for Enkidu is killed and Gilgamesh becomes morosely depressed, then going off in search of the secret of 'Eternal Life'. — However, as the core focus of this introduction (and volume) is the story of 'Adapa', we are not going to head any deeper into the stage-by-stage plotting of 'Gilgamesh' here.

What I would say, is that the multi-textured 'Gilgamesh' reads more like a bawdy tale of adventure, on a par with 'Beowulf', than a mature epic like Virgil's 'Aeneid'. It is a work that one can imagine being sung to a rowdy audience while eating and drinking — who are all so well acquainted with the ups and downs of Gilgamesh's exploits that they are able to follow the plot even while phasing in and out. I can imagine a bard delivering this eventful tale in song, and being just as inebriated, such that they would be in danger skipping or mixing up verses if they did not have some form of *aide-mémoire* as an antidote for the plot going "off the rails". All of the above is highly speculative, of course, but I believe it is essential to try and visualize the different ways in which these works from the past may have been performed or appreciated, instead of just viewing them as ossified works of literature, praising them as 'classics' and treating them as if they existed in a rarefied atmosphere of objectivity. I am not suggesting that any of the foregoing can be historically proven, but nor is it possible - on the basis of the incomplete knowledge that we still have of the day-to-day life of the Sumerians and subsequent inhabitants of the region - to disregard such hypothesizing as out of the question.

However, speculating any further on what *may have been* the modes of delivery or appreciation of 'Gilgamesh' will not help us in understanding its contemporary work 'Adapa', nor how it was a part of culture then, therefore let us shift our attention a bit.

Looking at the work of 'Adapa' - which existed in several forms over a period of at least two millennia - it does not make the same impression on me at all. For whereas 'Gilgamesh' seems like a popular and secular work (more like mass entertainment than literature), 'Adapa' comes across as a religious tale whose purpose goes beyond mere storytelling. My remarks are not based on reference to extensive research that has been undertaken into how and why the 'Adapa' story was written down, but on personal guesswork after reading the story countless times. What 'Adapa' seems to do, is not to offer us a gripping tale that leads us on from one set-piece to another, but rather to provide us with a narrative that offers explanations for several aspects of the world - at least of the world of the Sumerians and Akkadians. The key difference between deity and humanity is proposed therein, the power of words - both as curses and prayers - is explored, and (most importantly) the inception of the role of the exorcist, or magician, is laid out in the form of an explanatory 'origins story'.

'Adapa' is a very slender work in its length, certainly compared to 'Gilgamesh' - the former being akin to a short story, while the latter is like a novel. 'Adapa' is not a fiction work that requires a substantial amount of time to be told - true of 'Gilgamesh', with its many stages - but it is so compact in form that one can imagine it being performed in its entirety as part of some kind of religious celebration. We are reflecting on an age when fiction and religion were intimately combined. To tell the story of Jacob was to teach the Jews *about their religion*; in a similar way, to relate the story of Adapa was to explain to the Mesopotamian something *about the world that s/he lived in.* Somewhat like a 'theogony' - which explains the origins of Gods, as Hesiod did for the Greeks - the story of Adapa is *both fiction and religion*, the two not being divided from each other at that time.

Without being able to travel back there in something like H.G. Wells's Time Machine, it is not possible to say, for sure, how the words of the legend of 'Adapa' were recited or performed, so many years ago. While reading the fragments of 'Adapa' text, what impresses itself on my mind is the possibility that there were buildings whose purpose lay halfway between temples and theatres - where dramas like 'Adapa' may have been regularly enacted for the benefit of the people. However, I think that it may have been difficult to distinguish between what was the *general public* and *religious congregations* — for these might have been one and the same. I can visualize there having been players dressed up to represent the various characters that are portrayed in that work. The texts that have been passed down to us may be no more than the scripts of a drama that was frequently performed. I can imagine *Adapa's Ascent* (or whatever it was called) being presented somewhat like the *Mystery* (or *Miracle*) *Plays* of medieval Europe — in which the Bible stories are acted out as 'tableaux', with accompanying music or song, in religious settings. Just as scenes from the 'Creation', 'Adam and Eve', the 'Murder of Abel' and the 'Last Judgment' were displayed with actors dressed up as the key characters - not necessarily acting but visually representing scenes while words and music brought the *living pictures* to life - in a similar way I can imagine scenes of the 'Adapa' drama being presented to its ancient audience, words of the story recited as music plays, with costumed actors bringing each scene to life in a dramatic way.

The differences between the written versions of 'Adapa' (spanning two thousand years) is possibly the result of transformations in the way that the scenes of the drama were performed. Please note, I refer throughout this book to 'Adapa' as both a story and a drama - sometimes as a tale, myth or legend - as I think that it could have been *all these things* for the people to whom it clearly meant so much. Intricate studies have been undertaken, especially by Prof. Sara J. Milstein, into how scribes in Mesopotamia undertook the handing down of written texts - giving variable interpretations to literature through their editing work and the ways in which they presented a text. What I also find interesting is: if it *were true* that the tablets of 'Adapa' served the purpose of being the scripts for a drama - indicating *what was to be enacted* - do the places that we discover the 'Adapa' texts indicate the locations that this drama was performed, and does this indicate that Adapa was considered an important figure in all of those places — not only in Mesopotamia, but also Egypt and elsewhere?

It could be that I am grossly mistaken and that the 'Adapa' story was never performed in the way that I am imagining - however, what I am convinced of, is that 'Adapa' was always far more than just a text and that this story spread far and wide because it communicated something essential to Mesopotamians and others - each successive generation recognizing what was vital and archetypal in it, somewhat like 'Adam'. My overall viewpoint is that 'Adapa' is far more than just a group of clay tablets, more than a mere sequence of cuneiform symbols, but that it is up there with the first and foremost stories ever written - one still living and real, which has been immortalized in writing yet which is *so much more*.

The biggest difference between these examples of Mesopotamian literature, is that whereas the epic of 'Gilgamesh' has been available in mass-market editions (*e.g.* the 1960 Penguin translation) for over half a century and has featured in recommended lists of popular fiction for a long time, the epic of 'Adapa' has been unknown to the public at large and its study and appreciation has been almost entirely reserved to the scholarly communities. While 'Gilgamesh' has been a major influence upon dozens of works - writings, music, films, video games, even a Marvel comic character - 'Adapa' has been all but unknown outside of academia. In fact, prior to the current translation of *Adapa's Ascent*, no stand-alone volume - intended for the general public - previously existed.

# IV. MIGHTY HERO

*"The mighty hero of extraordinary powers,*
*able to lift Mount Govardhan on a finger"*
JOSEPH CAMPBELL

ADAPA IS PRESENTED AS A PERSON who can do anything - a fisherman, hunter, craftsman, priest, a leader of his people, even one who prepares food for worship. He appears as one who is skilled in almost everything, but above all he is described as *"Most Wise"*, and it is this epithet which attached itself to his name long before any of the written versions of the story that form the basis of *Adapa's Ascent.*

Adapa is the hero of this myth, and as in most mythical stories, he is made to appear larger than life. Whether the actual figure called "Adapa" once lived, or his character was a distillation from the lives of a number of individuals, is not a topic for which there is time (or sufficient evidence) to discuss here. It would, of course, be incredible to discover documentary evidence at some point that a real person called 'Adapa' existed, but we do not possess that yet. Instead, I would like us to take an initial look at the narrative of the 'Adapa' texts and in what way its central character is the hero of that drama. As we do so, I would like to make a few reflections on the distinction between Adapa and the other characters in that story — whilst also considering how its drama compares with other epic works and hero narratives.

*What is the plot of the 'Adapa' myth then?* -
If I were a budding screenwriter - and I had to deli-
ver my pitch of 'Adapa' to a movie producer in an ele-
vator with no more than forty words to do so - then
my one-sentence sell of the story would go something
like this: "*It's the tale of a man whose misuse of his
superpowers gets him called before God in Heaven -
and though he's offered the Gift of Immortality, his
father tricks him into turning it down and he is banished to Earth*". It sounds like a really exciting story,
even from such a simple, boiled-down synopsis, but
the narrative is a bit more complicated than this and
the devil is in the detail. If you haven't lost interest
by this point, then let me set out some more details
of the story, its key elements and core characters.

Adapa is described as a leader of his people,
possessing supreme qualities (physical and spiritual),
looking after them perfectly by fulfilling all of his
duties: feeding them, teaching them, leading his people
in worship, and much more. However, one day when
he is out fishing for them, his sailing-boat is capsized
by the might of the South Wind (Ninlil) and he is so
enraged, after almost having been drowned in the sea,
that he curses this Goddess — *so successfully* that she
ends up being rendered powerless for seven full days.

The loss of Ninlil's power does not go unnoticed in the Heavens, for Anu - 'Father of the Gods'
and the Supreme Force in the Mesopotamian Universe - learns that Adapa was the one who silenced

the South Wind with his words. Anu commands that this mortal be brought before Him and Adapa makes his way to Heaven — although not without receiving some advice from his father beforehand. Enki, also known as the 'God of the Deep [The Waters]', gives his son Adapa the grave warning that he is not to accept the "Food and Water of Death" when he is offered them by Anu in Heaven. As Enki is his native God - and also his father - he takes this advice seriously.

When Adapa arrives in Heaven and is offered the Food and Water by Anu - just as predicted by Enki - he heeds his father's warning and turns them down. However, the reality is that what Adapa had actually been offered was Food and Water *of Life* — and as a result of refusing these gifts Adapa has, in effect, openly shunned the gift of Immortality itself.

Anu immediately casts him out of Heaven - for if Adapa is only prepared to be a mere mortal, then he does not belong with the Immortal Gods. And this is where the generally accepted version of the myth of 'Adapa' ends. If you look up the story in encyclopedias and on websites, the preceding description is about as much as you will be told of the plot.

However, somewhat like a DVD with alternative endings, there are at least two other ways in which 'Adapa' can conclude - with the ending to the plot being dependent on which tablets you are reading. These, however, are beyond what I wish to consider in the present section. I would like to take a moment to look at the best-known ending, described above.

The storyline of Adapa being banished from Heaven by Anu - because of his rejecting the gift of Immortal Life - is an essential part of every version, and it tells us a lot about the Mesopotamian distinction between humans and Gods. In fact, it may have been created in order to explain just that.

The question of *what distinguishes Gods from Humankind* is one that is inextricably bound with the stories that are recounted in the Old Testament, the Greco-Roman epics and Mesopotamian epic poetry - to name just three sources of hero narratives. It is so omnipresent that it as if the search for the distinction between humanity and deity is a unifying theme that binds these traditions together in spite of their extremely wide divergences from each other.

'Exodus', 'The Odyssey', 'Gilgamesh' and 'The Aeneid' (to give just four examples), each has its own individual hero with their personal quests, vastly different from each other. Yet in spite of this, their protagonists have one thing in common: each of the heroes - whether Moses, Odysseus, Gilgamesh or Aeneas - has a relationship with the God or Gods who is at the heart of their story, ruling their world. This interaction - sometimes an actual dialogue - of the hero with their God or Gods, is something that forms an intimate and integral part of these epic narratives.

In the Pentateuch, for example, there are numerous figures with an heroic status, each of whom has a connection with 'Yahweh' (*"I Am that I Am"*)

- the God who wishes them to make His people leave behind their evil ways and bind to a Holy Covenant. Abraham, Noah, Moses and Joseph are heroes of a comparable kind to those that we find in 'The Odyssey' and 'Aeneid'. The difference is that whereas the Jewish heroes engage in an ongoing dialogue with their **one** Supreme God, the Greco-Roman heroes communicate with a whole congregation of Gods on their journeys - Zeus, Poseidon, Apollo, Hades *et al.*

Returning to the Mesopotamians, we find a scenario that is a combination of the Biblical and the Homeric, for there **is** one *All-Powerful God* in the world of Adapa and Gilgamesh - namely Anu - but there are also numerous lesser Gods, each of whom has strictly delimited areas of governance.

The drama of 'Adapa' is all about interaction with the Gods, for apart from Adapa's people - who are only mentioned indirectly - all of the characters with whom Adapa interacts are divine in some way.

Enki, for example - one of the key triumvirate of characters in 'Adapa' - is Adapa's father at the same time as being the 'God of Wisdom'. And there are not only dialogues between the protagonist and the Gods, but between the Gods themselves. — Enki, it appears, is engaged in a quiet power struggle with Anu, trying to prove that he has enough power to control his son's actions, even when he visits Anu, 'Lord of Heaven'. Ninlil too - God of the South Wind - is at the basis of the story, while Dumuzi and Gizzida are two other crucial Gods with whom Adapa interacts.

When Adapa appears, at the beginning of the story, he is a powerful individual who is clearly in charge of the world his people live in. He is presented as a wise and mighty mortal who is set above all those that he leads. However, the drama ultimately teaches us that the resounding difference between humans and Gods is one that applies to Adapa also: for one who does not accept Immortality cannot be on the same level as the Gods. Because Adapa rejects Immortal Life - albeit unwittingly - he relegates himself to remaining human. It is as if the whole purpose of the story is to provide us with an explanation as to why Gods live forever and humans only for a finite time — *it is because Adapa rejected the gift of Immortality*, therefore even though he was a supreme leader among mortals, he is not able to give *Immortal Life* to humans because he did not even accept it for himself. That is one perspective we can take on the story. We will consider others later on.

Even though it is not epic in its scale, I think that 'Adapa' has a character and story of genuinely heroic stature. *True* - the main actor does not have the grandeur of Gilgamesh, the courage of Odysseus or the sheer tenacity of Beowulf; *true* - there is no great sequence of heroic actions (as in the epics of the three characters named above); *true* also - nor is it sweeping in its scope, covering vast periods of time and space, like the Indian 'Mahabharata', the 'Icelandic Sagas' or even Leo Tolstoy's 'War and Peace'.

However, even though it is diminutive in size - the events covered in its narrative taking place in only a few days and in less space than a short story by Maupassant - 'Adapa' does appear to fulfill the requirements of epic literature. Taking the definition of 'epic' in 'Webster's International Dictionary', it seems to me that 'Adapa' ticks almost every box.

'Epic' is there described as: "*a [long] narrative poem (as Homer's Iliad) recounting heroic deeds set against a background of war and the supernatural, having a serious theme developed in a coherent and unified manner, written in a dignified style, and marked by certain formal characteristics [etc.]*".

*Firstly*, though many epics are indeed "long", even 'Gilgamesh' is no longer than a Henry James novella ('The Turn of the Screw') or a mini-novel like Steinbeck's 'Of Mice and Men', what *is true* of 'Adapa' (and 'Gilgamesh' too) is that it can definitely be described as a "narrative poem" - where the story of the main character is related in a poetic format.

*Secondly*, although there are no elements of war in 'Adapa' (as per the definition), there is nonetheless *conflict with the Gods* and it *is true* that the plot recounts, "heroic deeds set against a background of the supernatural". To paralyze the powers of a God - as Adapa does with Ninlil - categorizes as 'heroic' and the backdrop of the drama as a whole is quite obviously 'supernatural', for Gods govern Everything.

*Thirdly*, as for presenting us with a "serious theme developed in a coherent and unified manner",

I think that the theme of *Immortality* is one which forms a unifying thread that draws together the elements of the story. I don't feel as if it is a mere afterthought to the drama but that it is the 'serious theme' at its heart. It is, in fact, so closely bound together with the theme of *what distinguishes humans from Gods* — that these are like two sides of a single coin.

*Lastly,* in terms of being cast in a "dignified style" - the final defining characteristic mentioned by 'Websters' - I think that, on one hand, the semi-religious tone throughout does give a consistently noble tenor to the way that 'Adapa' is told. On the other, the serious style of the poetry alone elevates the level of writing in a way that prose so rarely achieves.

Though 'Websters' also refers to "certain formal characteristics" being common to epics, it does not specify these. Perhaps these would include the use of prophecies (or warnings) predicting the events later in the drama, the repetition of exact vocabulary between scenes (for example, in the language foretelling events and the actual unrolling of events) - in which case, 'Adapa' *does also include* features like that.

For me, in spite of its tiny length - taking up little more than forty pages of generously spaced verse - everything about 'Adapa' shouts out that it is an epic : *The Mortal Hero who rejects the gift of Eternal Life offered to him by his Supreme God, who is then banished from Heaven to Earth so as to complete his Life as a Mere Mortal* — what plot, be it short or long, could be grander in spirit and more awe-inspiring?

1

It is the simplicity of the plot which I believe makes it so gripping: at its heart is nothing less than the primal conflict between Gods and Humankind. Originally, my subtitle for this book was 'An Epic Fragment', because I believed that in spite of its size, it was unquestionably an epic for all the reasons that I have enumerated over the last couple of pages.

There is one more reason, however, that I think 'Adapa' is both *mighty* and *epic* - so worthy of being included in the pantheon of the great works of literature. This is that it is one of the first works ever to be written with a keen sense of the fundamental epic theme - puzzlingly nowhere mentioned in 'Websters' definition of an 'epic' - that of *Destiny*. This, in my belief, is the most common defining feature of all epics — the idea that there is a path of action which has been predetermined, and **must be followed** (even though it may be erred from), whether this has been set down by a God or Gods, revealed in dreams or has entered the hero's consciousness in any other way.

Whether we are talking about Luke Skywalker in 'Star Wars', Jason in Apollonius's 'Argonautica' or Väinämöinen in the Finnish 'Kalevala', it is the unwritten *Destiny* pursued by their heroes - whether it be attained or not - which I believe is the feature that brings these works together as 'epics'. Defeat of the "Dark Side of the Force", attainment of the 'Golden Fleece' or simply the finding of a suitable wife — *Destinies* can be as varied as you like, but they are what drive the stories ineluctably onwards.

As we shall see - once we turn to the continuation of the 'Adapa' drama beyond the *standard version*, wherein he is condemned to mortality - Adapa's ultimate destiny **is** 'Immortality': that theme of such grandeur which makes this epic so breathtaking.

The reason why Adapa is so significant as a '***hero***', is because he represents one of the first and purest attempts to depict a human as a 'superhero'. He is - like Gilgamesh and many Greco-Roman heroes to follow (Achilles, Perseus, Hercules, Aeneas, *et al.*) - the *Son of a God* and therefore exists on that tightrope of possibility between humanity and deity.

It is not the possession of any particular 'superpower' (for example, the power to strike down the 'South Wind') that makes the hero Adapa so 'mighty' in the story. To my mind, it is the *constant proximity of his character to becoming immortal* that makes this epic - and its key character - so powerful. In Heaven, he arrives at the crossroads of Eternity, and the question is whether he will follow the advice that he has been given or ignore it— seize Eternal Life or lose it.

Though there is little evidence that the Mesopotamians theorized about the nature of the 'hero' in the ways that we have since, Adapa finds himself *at the birth of the creation of heroes* and is as elemental - and flawed - as Adam and Lancelot, Noah and Neo. Now we have arrived at this point, the perspective from which I would like to consider Adapa is not so much in terms of his numerous abilities, but rather in terms of the 'Fatal Flaw' that defines him as a *Hero.*

# V. MIGHTY FALLEN

*"The beauty of Israel is slain upon thy
high places: how are the mighty fallen!"*
SECOND BOOK OF SAMUEL

THE FATAL FLAW OF LIFE IS DEATH - No-one
can ever alter that. However, fiction authors can do
their best to hide it, and what is impossible in reality,
the heroes of stories may accomplish. Though man is
mortal, a hero can become immortal - *and in which-
ever way our author chooses*. In the case of 'Adapa',
we have a proto-hero in possession of many of the
key traits of the character of the classic 'hero' that
would develop over the four millennia that followed.

Adapa is the survivor of a great disaster in the
form of colossal floods; he is a revered leader of his
people, and he has the power to strike down Gods
with the power of his words — shown by his stilling
the South Wind for seven whole days. It does not
matter that he does not have the physical prowess of
Gilgamesh - he has the power to defeat his foe without even lifting a finger, somewhat like Dr. Strange.

Sure, *strength* can be the powerful quality of
heroes and superheroes, from Hercules to Wonder
Woman, being one of the most obvious ways in which
the hero can demonstrate their might. That is why it is
particularly interesting that the authors of the myth of
'Adapa' have presented us with a hero far more powerful
than one who only conquers with strength. 'Adapa'

does not *just* present us with its main character as possessing superpowers, but each of its Gods as well. — Ninlil, who we meet first of all, does possess *physical strength* to the degree that she has the ability to blow with such enormous power that she can sink a boat with a single breath. Crucially, it is her capsizing of Adapa in this way - almost drowning his boat - which instigates Adapa to take revenge on her. Enki, on the other hand, one of two very powerful Gods introduced in this drama, does not demonstrate physical strength but *mental powers*. Among other abilities, Enki is able to see into the Future - like the Oracle or Cassandra in Greek Myth. He foresees what Adapa will be offered in Heaven; he predicts precise conversations Adapa will have on his way. The question is: *can he predict everything* or is there a point where human freedom can thwart his clairvoyance?

Anu, presented as the Supreme God in the universe of the Mesopotamians, has different powers still — as 'Father of the Gods' (occupying an analogous position to Kronos, the male progenitor of the Greco-Roman Gods). Anu is not only a creator of Gods who already exist, but he appears to have the power to turn a mortal into a God - which is what he offers Adapa. This makes Anu not just the holder of power, but the giver of powers. He represents the source of *All Power*, if you like - a very guardian of Power itself, though Mesopotamians do not describe it that way. What happens in the dramas of these early Gods is little different than what happens in DC or Marvel.

Gilgamesh may be a more typical hero - with his physical strength, his sexual prowess and his obvious competitiveness - but for that reason he is also a less interesting hero than Adapa. It is easy to see his positive qualities just as easy as it is to understand his quest in that epic: his need to beat Enkidu, afterwards their joint aim of vanquishing Humbaba, and then ultimately Gilgamesh's quest to discover the secret of Eternal Life. In that epic everything is clear and more obvious. We can understand Gilgamesh in the way that we can connect with modern heroes. We can see what his faults are as easily as his strengths.

Adapa is different than Gilgamesh, insofar as we are not presented with his motivation and his aims. We see how he is fooled into rejecting the gifts of Immortal Life, yet there was no point at which it was clarified *whether he wanted* Immortal Life. In the end, *it shall be his*, even though no scene in the drama presents him expressing any wish to have it, while Gilgamesh - who craves Immortal Life more than anything - will be doomed not to possess it, as he obtains it but it slips helplessly out of his grasp.

Before we proceed to look at *what happens next* - in the alternate endings - I want to consider for just a moment longer the powers and weaknesses of the characters in 'Adapa'. We will make no more reference to 'Gilgamesh' from here on, but focus entirely on the inner workings of the 'Adapa' drama alone. My purpose is simply to open some doors of consideration - things for you to think about as you read it.

"      The drama of 'Adapa' has most recently been entitled 'Adapa and the South Wind' by Prof. Shlomo Izre'el, the world's leading expert in all the cuneiform tablets on which it is based. That title is really helpful as it directs us to a very important aspect of the story - which is that the events of 'Adapa' all stem from a pivotal interaction between the main character and Ninlil (the South Wind), whom Adapa curses.

Whatever the powers of the South Wind, that were known of by Sumerians and Akkadians in terms of assisting the growth of crops or fishing with boats - in the light of Adapa's ability to bring down Ninlil with a single curse, it is clear that the South Wind is not a flawless God. Adapa is a mortal and therefore the South Wind's susceptibility to a human curse could certainly be counted among its fatal flaws. While in Achilles's case, an *arrow* to the heel can mean death, in Ninlil's case, *words* from Adapa's mouth spell downfall.

The question is — *what is Adapa's own weakness?* To this I think there are at least two answers - though I will be very interested to hear from any readers who identify flaws different from those that I mention here. In the first instance, I think that Adapa's inability to let go of the episode with Ninlil capsizing his boat, casting a curse in his rage, is in itself a flaw. Like Marvel's character 'Thor', Adapa has a similar short temper and acts in a "hot-headed way" when he curses Ninlil. Then again, without this 'flaw' there would no drama — for Adapa would not be so strictly summoned to appear before Lord Anu.

However, on a larger scale, there seems to me to be a more obvious flaw of Adapa's - one which I would call either 'gullibility' or 'tractability'. I say this because the direction that the drama follows is determined by how Adapa does not make an unaffected decision of his own at the moment that a vital choice is set before him, but he goes along with what he has been counselled to do by his father, the God Enki. While in Superman's case it is a material object, external to himself, which is able to sap him of all his powers - in the form of the mineral Kryptonite - with Adapa it is an internal, psychological trait, which leads to him losing the greatest gift that could possibly be offered to him - that of *Eternal Life itself.*

If Adapa were not so influenced by what his father had told him, not so willing to believe that what the 'God of Wisdom' told him was true, he might have actually accepted the gifts of the 'Water of Life' and the 'Food of Life'. Though my opinion is that he is behaving like an overtrusting son, maybe I am too hasty to label this as *'Gullibility'.* Maybe what Adapa has is simply *'Respect'* — respect for his father and respect for a God who is in a higher position of power than himself. However, does that mean that he needs to take all this advice on trust and act according to his father's best ideas, and not according to what he feels in his own heart it is best to do?

Maybe I have identified two possible flaws of Adapa's - though whether you agree with me or not is immaterial, for I think that nothing is more vital (in appreciating fiction) than arriving at your own points-of-view independently. In the same way that I secretly wish that Adapa had come to his own, un-influenced decision regarding the acceptance or de-clining of the gifts he was offered - I also earnestly wish for you to come to your own personal views of what you believe is happening in the 'Adapa' epic.

Whether you see Adapa's fate as determined by his brashness, his trusting nature or actually the fault of his father Enki alone - for lying to him unfairly - you can consider different interpretations each time that you read it. The reality is that the drama of 'Adapa' can never be to us what it was to the Meso-potamians. For them, it is quite likely that 'Adapa' was far more than "just a story". In the same way that those of various faiths go to churches and temples nowadays, with firm conviction that their religions explain something about the world they live in and give them a moral compass — in a similar way the stories of Adapa and other figures gave meaning to the world of the Sumerians, Akkadians and others. Now, however, their entire civilizations have disappeared, and it is not possible for us to appreciate what those stories meant to their cultures so many thousands of years ago. We can try, but we are almost inevitably destined to fail. In the light of that, I think that it is preferable for us to ask *what we can gain* from the stories ourselves - to look for what truths they can give to our lives - to search for *personal meanings*.

# VI. THE HUMAN CONDITION

*"Escape from*
*the human condition,*
*I am telling you, is not powerful,*
*but all-powerful"*
ANDRÉ MALRAUX

TO ESCAPE FROM BEING HUMAN — is that why we wish to lose ourselves in worlds of fiction? Was that the *raison d'être* of stories from the start? To forget about *mortality* and focus on *Immortality* is, I guess, one way in which a human being can abandon its mere humanness, *even if only imaginarily.* Eternal Life - at the core of 'Adapa' and 'Gilgamesh' - is the topic which, more than any other, leads the mortal reader to let his or her mind wander free from temporal constraints. They can imagine, like the Gods and heroes presented to them, being emancipated from *Death.*

In the version of 'Adapa' that we have looked at up to now, Adapa is ejected from Heaven by Anu the instant that he turns down the gifts of the *Food and Water of Life.* Adapa is sent back to his place on Earth, for only Immortals can live with Gods — those who reject immortality must remain human.

However, it appears that the Mesopotamians had a rethink of this ending as time passed, and certainly by the 7th Century BCE we discover an alternate possibility for the closure of the 'Adapa' drama - one that is recorded in a number of tablet fragments.

*Version Two* of the 'Adapa' myth shows us something most intriguing. It appears that after a moment of deeper thought, Anu has realized that Adapa was poorly advised by his father Enki, perhaps even tricked. Giving consideration to the fact that it is probably not Adapa's fault for having rejected the gifts of Immortality - but due to Enki's overly insistent advice - Anu chooses to make a new decision, reversing the one he had previously made. In some brand new passages, Anu's irritation with Enki is recorded and the 'God of Gods' decides to welcome Adapa into Heaven — *Immortal with the Gods*.

This is an amazing turn of events, a complete about-face of the plot - who could predict this would take place? It is worth observing that in the earliest versions of 'Adapa' - dating from the 18th Century BCE - not only is Adapa thrown out of Heaven for his refusal, but it is Enki as much as Adapa who must *answer for* and *put right* the things that are of concern to Anu.

However, it is clear in the more-or-less complete version of the story that is recorded in the 14th Century BCE tablets, that Adapa is unquestionably thrown out of Heaven because of his rejection of the gifts offered by Anu. So, the changes of narrative are clearly a gradual development, and it is impossible for us to know - without any other intervening texts - how long it took for the mutations in plot to take place. Maybe there had been a sense, in the audiences who became familiar with the story over many centuries, that it just wasn't fair that Adapa should take the fall for succumbing to Enki's bad advice. What appears most fascinating to me is that whereas *before*, Anu was unwilling to have mercy - in spite of Adapa explaining that he had only followed Enki's advice - *now* there seems to be something like *Redemption* for him. I am not suggesting that the idea of 'redemption', in the Christian sense, had come to maturity by then, but at least the idea of giving someone a second chance - in this case Adapa - does take place in this story.

Conceding that Adapa's refusal was as much due to Enki's parental pressure as due to his own will is a truly interesting element, for this shows that the Akkadians took the notion of 'Responsibility' seriously. Not only does it appear essential for them to consider *who has undertaken an action* in order to determine who is responsible, but in the instance of 'undue influence' - which is what some might consider Enki to be applying - it is *the one who has applied that influence who is partly responsible for the actions* that have been committed. It would be intriguing to consider legal cases from this period, to see to what extent judgments took into account *undue influence of misleading advice* on a person being prosecuted for a crime: did this ever count as 'mitigating' and result in some degree of mercy in the punishment?

Returning to 'Adapa' though, I think that the change in the narrative quite likely points to the evolution in mentality of the audiences as well. Whereas before, the banishment of Adapa from Heaven had been a totally acceptable fate for him to suffer, the public may have developed to a point where that is no longer seen as proportionate to his actions. Looking at modern audiences of movies and television series, I think that it is relevant to observe that once we have become too familiar with a certain type of plot, it is essential for screenwriters to introduce changes, or our attention will be lost. An audience can be so totally conversant with every single aspect of a genre - for example, the *thriller* - that unless some new directions of action are explored, viewers will become apathetic to the events being portrayed — repetition must be accompanied by some sort of variation.

I am not saying that a deliberate decision was made - on a certain day - to change or add to the plot in the way that we witness it transforming in the 7th Century BCE. Rather, I think that there was a gradual shift in attitude, from one where Adapa's ejection from Heaven was entirely acceptable and congruent with the theology of the day, to a point where the majority of the public had developed some sympathy with Adapa's fate — *and Enki's partial responsibility for it* — to the extent that a dénouement in which Adapa would be allowed to re-enter Heaven became the preferable one, and grew from the previous version as a natural extension of that drama.

What both of the versions do abide by, is a *Logic of Deity and Immortality*: **if** you are to be a God, **then** you must have Immortality — **if** you do not have Immortal Life, **then** you cannot be a God. - These principles are true of the two versions of the plot that have been set forth up to here. Adapa is excused for his error, it is true, but he is given Immortality by Anu so that he can enter Heaven. What is curious - yet might be answered by new artifacts in future - is that Adapa's name has not been discovered in any list of persons who have been deified, while Gilgamesh (it is recorded) was turned from a *king* into a *God*.

Was Adapa not considered to have become a God, in spite of his entering Heaven? Was he seen as being a 'Special Case' - *neither human nor God* - yet nonetheless residing in Heaven with the Immortals? As it is not possible for me to provide any helpful answer to this query, it is time for us to move on.

It is clear, from both the earliest and latest tablets bearing the tale of 'Adapa', that the narrative was seen as more than a mere story and that there was a purpose to telling it that went far beyond entertaining an audience. Whereas in the case of 'Gilgamesh', there are many narrative devices that indicate that the story was being recited to an avid audience, what is evinced by the 'Adapa' texts is that there was a purpose to the tale that can best be described as 'religious'.

There is a *third way* in which 'Adapa' ends, and it is true of the earliest complete version (c. 1760 BCE) as also of the most recent fragments (c. 7th C. BCE). Over a period spanning more than a thousand years, there is evidence that the 'Adapa' narrative closed with a prayer, or incantation. This third ending is perhaps the one that is of most significance.

In the original Sumerian version there is a prayer appended to the poem, one which humans are to use in order to be cured of illness. The names of various Gods are invoked, including Adapa's father 'Ea'. However, by the seventh century BCE the invocation with which 'Adapa' closes had become more intriguing, for it provides us with the brief account of an illness that kills off many people, something like a plague (at least that is how I have interpreted it). There is good reason for there to be an ending that is about Adapa curing humanity of illnesses — for Adapa, in his Immortality, has become a figure whose *name* is enough to be invoked in order to cast away sickness. It is as if, through attaining Immortal Life, he has become "*the master of all that ails men in their mortal lives*". The figure of Adapa develops into one that is synonymous with life and healing, and for that reason his very name became a verbal talisman to ward away all forms of physical evil - including illnesses of every kind.

What some versions of 'Adapa' close with can also be called a *spell* - and Adapa is viewed by some as the *First Magician* or *Proto-Exorcist*, existing even after his death. Even in the first part of the story of Adapa, we have been shown how words off his tongue alone are potent enough to bring down the mighty Ninlil. This ending of the plot supports the belief - which had become widespread - that *Adapa's name* was the surest, most effective way in which to drain power from illness, that uttering such an invocation was the best way to overcome the evil spirits that possessed someone.

In the late 1st Millennium BCE, it is possible to appreciate the kind of ritual to which the character of Adapa had become central by reading the text of the ʻUtukku Lemnutu Incantation', where it states: "— *As Adapa, sage of Eridu, I am Ea's incarnation priest, and I am Marduk's messenger. In order to cure the patient of his illness the Great Lord Ea sent me. He superimposed his incantation on mine, he superimposed his pure mouth upon mine, he superimposed his pure spittle on mine, he superimposed his pure prayer upon mine*". - You will notice that this passage is written in the first person. This is because the Mesopotamians believed that the one who performed the ritual *actually became like* **a reincarnation of Adapa himself** whilst performing those rites - that this was the reason why the exorcist would be successful in expelling demons from a person.

One can only try to imagine what such a ritual performance of the incarnation priest could have been like. Quite possibly, the person enacting the scene would have dressed up in the way that Adapa was represented in pictures and statues - though few of these have survived. It is possible that the priest who performed the ritual began speaking in a different voice, while following the exact words of an incantation like the one quoted. Quite possibly the rite was undertaken publicly, accompanied by music and incense, taking place only in certain prescribed locations, such as temples designated for the purpose. The more that we learn of Mesopotamia, the more we may be able to appreciate the exact way in which priests and exorcists performed their roles. We have uncovered a lot of evidence already but not enough to be able to boast that we know *exactly* what took place and how.

What it is essential for the modern reader to appreciate is that the myth of Adapa is not presenting some made-up world of Gods and Heaven written for entertainment purposes: a 'fairytale'. The Mesopotamian viewpoint on Adapa - as an influential religious figure - was a real and actual one, not just a fiction. They believed in his power to eradicate illness in the same way that we believe in the power of medicine to do so. While we believe in such unseeable forces as electricity and gravity, Sumerians and Akkadians believed in the invisible agencies of Gods. While for us, we base our world-view upon the combined theories of Profs. Isaac Newton, Albert Einstein and Stephen Hawking (to name a few) — for the people of Mesopotamia it was Anu, Enki, Ninlil and others (including Adapa) who were sufficient explanations of how the world works. They believed in the truth of their Gods with the same fervor and conviction that we believe in science's capacity to explain the cosmos.

Though there is a limit to how many times I can make a similar point without it becoming jaded and even irritating, what I urge you to appreciate while reading 'Adapa' - as deeply as you can - is that the various versions of this text represented a cornerstone of 'Truth' for those who were familiar with it

— that it was a part of their day-to-day reality just as newspapers and the internet are a part of our own.

1.5 Million Days have passed since the most recently recorded myth of 'Adapa'. Do we really all believe in things so different than what people believed in then? Has 'Magic' actually given way to 'Reason'? Are there not some of us who are still ready to believe in the exorcist's powers? — Casting a backward glance to the nearest past, are the days of religion's dominance really so distant? Miracles, blessings and cures - are these not something many believe in still? It is my opinion that we may not have progressed so very far beyond the Mesopotamians to lack appreciation for the way in which they believed in their Gods — there are billions of us who are still adherents of religions.

It is my personal belief that the line between fiction and non-fiction is really quite slender indeed. What interests me is not whether the librarian shelves a book on the 'Fiction' or 'Non-Fiction' section - but whether the book brings some truth and reality *to me*, the reader. Of course, 'Adapa' tells us a story, but to say it is "only fiction" does not tell us more about what it is. The reality is that 'Adapa' possessed **_truth_** for its audience (be they secular or religious) and it does not matter whether an actual 'Adapa' ever existed. In the same way that Jesus, Mohammed and Abraham are still real in their truth value to Christians, Muslims and Jews today — so equally was Adapa a figure of real significance at the core of the Mesopotamian's World.

## FINAL THOUGHTS
### on Gods & Mortals

WHEN I LOOK AT THE PLOT of the 'Adapa' texts from a bird's eye view, what I see is a tug-of-war between Enki and Anu to have control of its mortal hero. What is not as clear to me is *Why* - especially in the case of Enki - this conflict is so very important to win. The crux of this battle, of course, comes down to the moment when Adapa must make his choice. Offered the gifts of Food and Water in Heaven, Adapa chooses to do as his father says — and this, for just a moment at least, allows Enki to win his battle. Yet the truth is that this battle was unfairly won because Enki soweds seed of confusions by telling Adapa that he would be offered the Food and Water "*of Death*". All the words Enki spoke convinced Adapa that if he consumed them, then he would die. So he declined.

The only way in which one could say that Enki was telling the truth, is that *if* Adapa ate and drank the gifts that Anu offered him, *his mortality would die*, and like a mortal bitten by a vampire he would rise to a new life — one of eternal duration.

If only he were listening more closely, Adapa would notice that he is being offered gifts "*of Life*" and not the lethal ones that his father had predicted. What Enki accomplishes, though, is not only to control his son Adapa, but to frustrate Anu — who had clearly made a firm decision to offer Immortality to Adapa after seeing how powerfully he had "*cut off*

*Ninlil's wings*" with a single curse. What creates suspense, is that the way in which Adapa is summoned to Anu, we do not know whether the free-willed mortal will be reprimanded for his actions - or rewarded.

Enki obviously knew that in turning down gifts of Immortality, his son would not be able to become a God: so *why* did he not want his son to become like Him? We are given no indication. Was it simply a case of a father not wanting his son to become more powerful than him? Or did Enki, in all good faith, not want to burden his son with taking on the mantle of a 'God' — with that role of Eternal Responsibility?

What I find fascinating about the drama of 'Adapa', is that his turning down of Eternal Life is a decision made without really knowing what choice is in front of him. It is a key moment in World Literature: the mortal hero standing on the verge of Immortality, yet he does not realize this at all! The question is: would Adapa have accepted Immortal Life if he knew it was being offered to him?- *We will never know.*

To me, it seems much like a cosmic joke between the Gods, no less absurd than Kafka's 'K' turning up to court and not knowing the charges against him. Adapa is being treated as if he were a '*Plaything of the Deities*', nothing more. The reason for Anu's own anger, which is encountered in Chapters XIV-XV of this translation of *Adapa's Ascent*, is that Enki is not only treating Adapa like a human puppet, but he is treating Anu himself like a God who can be manipulated, and that is where Anu finally draws the line.

It is extremely difficult to bring a discussion of the multi-faceted and profound work of Mesopotamian Literature that is 'Adapa', to a satisfactory close. — The closer one peers into the depths of this drama, the more possibilities are uncovered and the more complicated it becomes. It may be the shortest of epics, but for my part, I find it unendingly rich, perhaps more than anything else due to the dynamic traits of its three core characters: Adapa, Anu and Enki. It is important to understand that these were as meaningful and relatable to the Mesopotamian of the First and Second Millennium BCE as Neo, Morpheus and Trinity are to us in the 21st Century. The difference is that while Sumerians and Akkadians recorded their stories on clay tablets, we now watch (rarely bother to read) our literature on electronic tablets. It is, nonetheless, my sincere hope that a new generation of readers will discover how rewarding it is to experience the full drama of *Adapa's Ascent*, irrespective of whether that be as a *Book* or *eBook*.

The topic of which story was actually written or told first is a rather vacant discussion. We cannot possibly know of what answers are buried beneath the earth; so many empty words are spoken about what we do not know. Though the 'Eridu Genesis' gives us an account of the Gods who birthed the Sumerian's universe, and thus it is a 'first story' in one crucial way, it could be that the first story ever written has nothing to do with the creation of the cosmos, like 'Gilgamesh' — which *is generally reputed* as being the 'first story'.

Whatever Gods or forces are named by a people as their Ultimate Creator (in the sense that they are *responsible for the creation of their cosmos*), be it the pantheon of Greek Gods, the God of Abraham or a Singularity, those who live and tell stories to each other are faced with the same apparent reality:— their lives are transient, whereas the world they have been born into (and will die in) seems as if it is something that will endure, irrespective of their own existences. The world around us seems to be *that which lasts*, while we are merely passers-through — *the evanescent*: Temporal lives lived in an Eternal Universe.

I sometimes contemplate that humankind's dawning consciousness of *Mortality* and *Immortality*, expressed in writing, may perhaps represent the most primordial type of story, more significantly than what merely came first in time. *Is there any difference more absolute than the dichotomy between what lasts for-ever and that which exists only for an instant?* — Adapa, mortal, presented as the first and ultimate leader of civilization, only becomes acutely conscious of his mortality after being thrown back to Earth from Heaven, for refusing the Water and Food of Eternal Life. Whether an edition of *Adapa's Ascent* (origi-nally translated as 'Adapa into Heaven') is ever un-earthed that predates even the earliest 'Gilgamesh' epic fragments, the truth is that what both these leg-endary works share, is that they keep the reader in true suspense as to whether Adapa, and Uruk's King, will ultimately gain *Immortality*, or die as mortals.

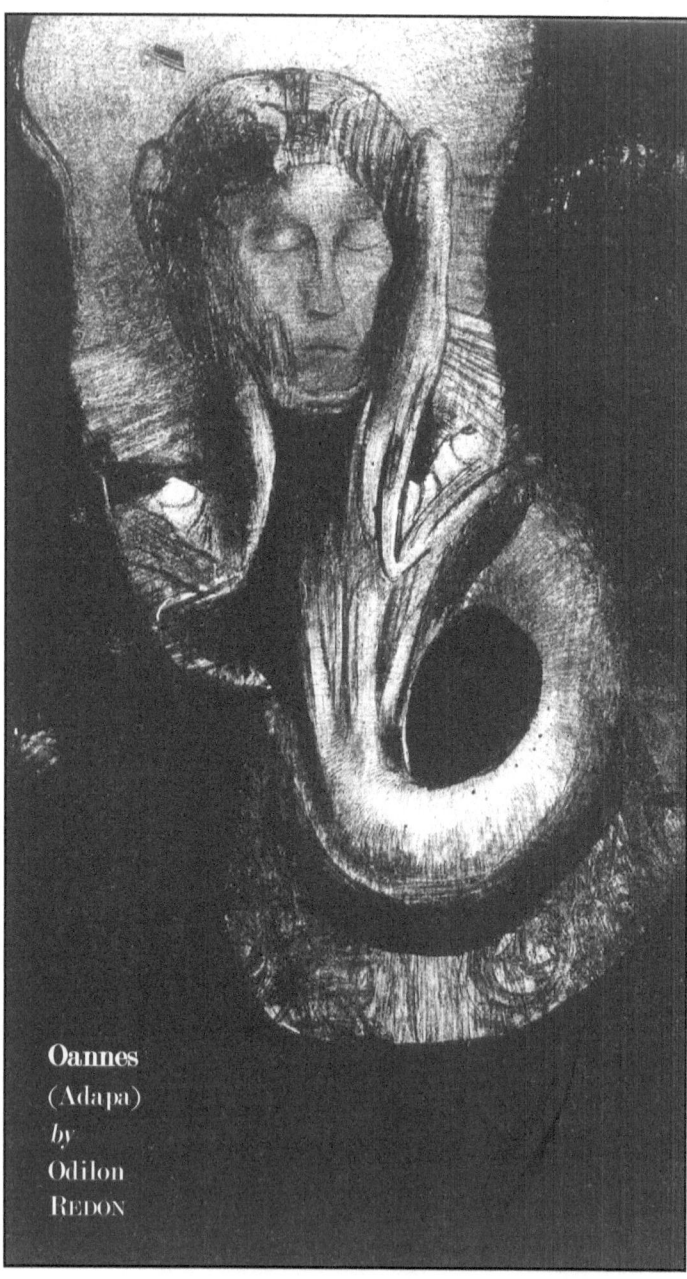

**Oannes**
(Adapa)
*by*
Odilon
Redon

# ADAPA's

# ASCENT

## A Myth of Man & IMMORTALITY

"*GILGAMESH WHERE ART THOU WANDERING?*
*THOU WILT NOT FIND THE LIFE THOU SEEKEST*
*- WHEN THE GODS THEY CREATED HUMANITY*
*DEATH WAS INSTILLED IN THE HUMAN SOUL*
*LIFE THEY KEPT FOR THEMSELVES*"

translated into
**English Verse**

*by*

# Edouard d'ARAILLE

- ADAPA -

Born of the Sea,

O So Wise One,

in ANU's Light

Do You Live

- ADAPA -

Flown to the Sky,

O So Pure One,

Eridu's Priest

A  FISH

become

BIRD

*WITH FATE NO MAN CAN INTERVENE*

# 0 *Prologue of* **Destiny**

*LET HIS WORDS*
*be filled*
*with*
*Learning* –

*Let his Speech,*
*like ANU's,*
*with*
*Power command*

*With Reason Great*
*did* **GOD** *create*
*him* –

*Revealing*
*to humans*
*the World's Design*

*To* **him**
*did ANU*
*Give His Wisdom* –

**but not** ETERNAL LIFE

# I **ADAPA of ERIDU**

AND IN THOSE DAYS
and years
did ENKI
make
this
Man
of Eridu
*The Sage*
a Guardian
of Mankind -

Speaking
like a Prophet,

none will dare
defy him

Adept
and deep in
Understanding,

like the Seven
DEITIES
is he -

*Pure in Heart*

*and*

*Clean of Hand,*

*Anointed is he*

*and*

*Observant of*

      *Holy Acts*

With the cooks

he performs

his tasks

like a cook -

like a cook

of this town,

he prepares

the fare

Daily

he offers

oblations for

Eridu - serving

its congregation


With hands

unstained

he sets

the table,

without him

the altar

shall not

be cleared


\*　　\*　　\*　　\*　　\*　　\*

## III  UPON the WIDE SEA

AND AT
THIS TIME
Adapa,
Eridu
born -

EA
lain
resting,
aslumber
in bed -

each day
would attend
to the gates
of the City

he bolts them,
unbolts them,
at dawn
and
at dusk

From the Sacred Port
like a crescent
moon shaped,
each morn
he embarks in
his sailing boat -

for the people
of Eridu
does he
fish, upon
the wide seas
he makes his catch

With no rudder
to guide him,
he drifts
along -

with no punt pole
to push with,
he steers
his craft

# Ⅲ ADAPA's DESCENT

ONE DAY AS HE
was catching
carp for his
LORD's House
- far out at sea -

NINLIL, the South
Wind, blew forth
with force,
the Waters
slicing in half - - -

The boat overturned
and Adapa
drowned,
in the home
of the fishes
submerged below

*- O his Heart
beat with Fury*

- - - **he Cursed
that South Wind!**

# IV  The POWER of WORDS

"*HOW DID I -*
*O SOUTH WIND,*
*destroy your*
*brothers? -*

*I broke off*
*their wings*
*with the Force*
*of my Words!*

*Just like them*

*- **I swear** -*

*I shall*

*break off*

*yours too with*

*a **Single Curse!**"*

AND THE MOMENT

THIS SPEECH

HAD COME

OUT OF

HIS MOUTH,

THE WINGS OF

THE SOUTH WIND

BROKE    ASUNDER

*AND*

*FOR*

*SEVEN*

*WHOLE*

*DAYS DID*

*THE SOUTH*

*WIND NOT BLOW*

*UPON THE LAND*

- - - - - - -

# $\mathbb{V}$ *"BRING THAT MAN HERE!"*

LORD
ANU,
HE
SUMMONED
His
vizier
Llabrat:

*"FOR*
*SEVEN*
*WHOLE DAYS*
*HAS THE SOUTH WIND*
*NOT BLOWN ON*
*MY LAND -*

*TELL*
*ME*

*WHY*
*IS THIS*
*SO?"*

- and
His minister
answered Him
straight away thus:

*"O My King,
it was **Adapa**
- Son of ENKI -
who broke off
the wings of
the Mighty
South Wind"*

Lord ANU, on
hearing this
shouted out:
*"SAVE HIM!"*

He rose from
His throne
and cried:

*"BRING
THAT MAN
HERE!"*

# VI  The PROPHECIES of ENKI  *Part the 1ˢᵗ*

ENKI,
KNOWING THE WAYS
of Heaven,
on Adapa He laid
His hands

He had
his hair appear unkempt
and made
his clothes like one bereft

- Then EA gave
counsel to Adapa,
spoke of the Future
and what he must do:

"Adapa,
you are to
visit King ANU -
shall enter His Palace
and meet with
Him there . . .

Once
you have
scaled the stairs
to the Skies - and

Once
you have
stepped toward
Lord ANU's gates -

DUMUZI
and GIZZIDA,
there shall they stand,

there will they see you
and of you
demand:

'YOU THERE!
FOR WHOM ARE
YOU TRANSFORMED THUS?

- ADAPA -
WHY NOW IN
GARMENTS OF GRIEF?'

**Answer**
**to them**
- you must
talk like this:

"*From my Land*
*two Gods left*
*and so sombre*
*I dress* - - -"

'WHO ARE THE GODS
WHO HAVE GONE?'
will they ask -

'DUMUZI
and GIZZIDA',
you must respond

\*      \*      \*      \*      \*      \*

*They shall look*
*into*
*each other's eyes -*
**and**
**at this will they smile**

Then

shall

they put

in a warm

word with ANU

and show you

a friendlier

face of

their

God"

## VII  BY ROYAL COMMAND

THE HERALD
OF ANU
arrived
afore
ENKI -

proclaiming
the message
his Master
had sent:

"THIS ADAPA - HE

WHO HAS BROKEN

THE WINGS OF

THE MIGHTY

SOUTH WIND

YOU MUST

SEND HIM

TO ME!"

## VIIII  The PROPHECIES of ENKI *Part the 2*[nd]

"AS YOU STAND
BEFORE ANU
to you shall
be offered
the *Food*
*of Death*

Heed
my words:
DO NOT EAT!


- stood there
before ANU
to you shall
be offered
the *Water*
*of Death*

Heed
my words:
DO NOT DRINK!

But when
you are
offered
some robes:

GET DRESSED!

And when
you are
offered
some oil:

ANOINT YOURSELF!

\*     \*     \*     \*     \*     \*

*DO NOT IGNORE*

*THIS ADVICE*

*THAT I GIVE*

*YOU - OBEY*

*OF MY WARNING*

*EACH  WORD!*"

# IX  JOURNEY to the GREAT ABOVE

SO
EA
SENT
ADAPA
on his way,
up the steps
that Ascend to
the GREAT ABOVE -

and once he arrived
at the Gateway of
ANU - DUMUZI
and GIZZIDA
waited
there

Both
of them
caught sight
of Adapa, calling:

"GOD HELP YOU,
YOUNG MAN! —

*FOR*
*WHOSE SAKE*
*ARE YOU CHANGED*
*LIKE THIS?*

ADAPA -
WHY WEAR
YOU ROBES OF
MOURNING?"

"- *My Land*
*two Gods left*
*and so thus*
*am I dressed*"

"BUT WHO ARE
THE GODS WHO
FROM YOUR LAND
HAVE FLED? -"

"*DUMUZI*
*and*
*GIZZIDA*"
Adapa said

*And they looked
into
each other's eyes -
**and**
**at this they smiled**!*

# X In the PALACE of KING ANU

AS ADAPA
DREW NEAR
King ANU's
Being  - - - -
the Lord of Gods
saw him and
called out:

"COME HERE!

COME HERE
AND TELL ME,
DEAR ADAPA,
WHY DID YOU
BREAK OFF
THE WINGS
OF THAT
MIGHTY
SOUTH
WIND?" -

ANU's query
did Adapa
answer
at once:

"MY KING,

that day as I
was catching
carp for my
LORD's Temple
- far out at sea -

NINLIL, the South
Wind, blew forth
with force,
the waters
slicing in half - - -

The boat overturned
and so was I
drowned
in the home
of the fishes
submerged below

- *O my Heart
beat with Fury*

- - - *I Cursed
that South Wind!*"

DUMUZI
and GIZZIDA
stood beside him
- to ANU his side
of the story
reciting

\*     \*     \*     \*     \*     \*

As
ANU,
He heard it,
His heart
it did
calm

PURE

SILENCE

HE BECAME

# XI "WHY?"

"*WHY DID EA*
*LET SUFFER*
*THIS MAN*
*WHAT IS*
*HEINOUS*
*IN HEAVEN*
*AND EARTH?*

*WHY DID*
*ENKI MAKE*
*ADAPA LOSE*
*HIS HEAD -*
*AND BEHAVE*
*IN THIS WAY*
*SO BRASH?*

**ENKI**
IS HE
WHO
HAS
DONE
THIS TO
ADAPA! -

*HOW CAN WE*
*HELP HIM NOW?*"

# XII - GIFTS IMMORTAL -

THEN

ANU

SAID:


"BRING

TO

HIM

THE

FOOD

OF

LIFE

THAT

HE

MAY

EAT

IT"


\*     \*     \*     \*     \*     \*

To
Adapa
was brought
the **Food of Life** -

*HE WOULD NOT EAT IT*

To
Adapa
was brought
the **Water of Life** -

*HE WOULD NOT DRINK IT*

Yet
when he
was brought
out some clothes -

*HE DRESSED*

and
when he
was brought
out an ointment -

*ANOINTED HIMSELF*

LORD ANU,

He looks on

this *human* and

then He just

laughs and

He asks:


*"COME NOW,*

*DEAR ADAPA!*

**WHY DID YOU**

**NEITHER EAT**

**NOR DRINK?"**

## XIII  BANISHED from the HEAVENS

"FROM THIS DAY ON
ETERNAL LIFE
SHALL NOT
BE YOURS -

O WOE BETIDE,
**MERE MORTALS!**"

\*     \*     \*     \*     \*     \*

"DEAR ANU -
**HAVE MERCY!**
for ENKI
my Father
He warned me before:

'*DO NOT EAT
WHAT YOU ARE GIVEN!*

*DO NOT DRINK
WHAT IS OFFERED TO YOU!*'"

But
ANU,
though
hearing
this,
*made*
*His*
*Decree*:

"**TAKE HIM**
**AWAY**
**FROM ME!**

**SEND HIM**
**HENCE**
**BACK TO**
**HIS WORLD!**

**- - - FOR HE**
**DOES NOT**
**BELONG**
**HERE**
**WITH**
**GODS**
**IMMORTAL!**"

## XIV - DEAR ENKI -

YET WHEN ANU
HEARD
Adapa's
heart
in its torment

He sent back
His envoy
to EA,
enquiring:

" - DEAR ENKI - YOU
WITH CLEAR THINKING
BLESSED, WHO KNOW
GREAT GODS, THEIR
HEARTS WITHIN -

YOU WHO OBSERVE
US LORDS OF HEAVEN,
WHO KNOW HOW TO
REACH ME, YOUR
KING SUPREME -

WHAT DID YOU
ORDER YOUR SON
SHOULD DO? WHY
DID YOU SEND ADAPA
- *MORTAL* - TO ME?


- DEAR ENKI - YOU
WITH CLEAR THINKING
BLESSED, WHO KNOW
GREAT GODS, THEIR
HEARTS WITHIN -


IF YOU WANTED TO
FIND HIM A PLACE
IN THE HEAVENS, WHY
SEND HIM TO ME IN
MOURNING DRESSED?


- FOR YOU ORDERED
HIM WEAR HIS HAIR
UNCOMBED, HIS LIMBS
TO BE BALMED AND BE
SMEARED WITH ASH!

- FOR YOU BADE HIM :

'*ADAPA, YOU ARE*
*TO VISIT KING ANU*

*AND WHEN YOU*
*DO MEET HIM*
*MY WORDS*
*MUST OBEY !* -

*ONCE*
*YOU HAVE*
*SCALED THE STAIRS*
*TO THE HEAVENS     AND*

*ONCE*
*YOU HAVE*
*STEPPED TOWARD*
*LORD ANU'S GATES*

*DUMUZI*
*AND GIZZIDA*
*THERE SHALL THEY STAND*

*THERE SHALL THEY*
*MEET YOU*

*AND* **THIS**
*I COMMAND . . .*' "

# XV *"WHO AMONG GODS?"*

AT THE ACTIONS OF
ENKI
did ANU laugh loud
and He
scolded Him much:

"WHO AMONG GODS
IN THE HEAVENS
AND EARTH - JUST
AS MANY THEY BE -
COULD HAVE BEEN
OH SO FOOLISH TO
DO SUCH A THING?

WHO AMONG GODS
COULD BETHINK
HIS OWN WORDS

*MORE*
*ALMIGHTY*
*THAN MINE?* -

**THE**
**LORD**
**SUPREME!**"

# XVI ADAPA's ASCENT

AND SO

ANU MADE

Adapa rise -

from the skin of

the Earth to the eye

of the Sky - while

beholding HIS

RADIANCE

*BLINDED*

IN AWE

Adapa
then did
Lord ANU
Appoint to
His Service,
from ENKI
Set Free -
*Now and*
*Always*

The LORD
ABSOLUTE
did Ordain that
the Wisdom and
Power Triumphant
of Adapa *Ever*
*E t e r n a l*
*Be Seen*

# XVII  'SO BE IT'

*SO DID ADAPA*

*Vital Seed*

*of Humankind*

*- He who broke off*

*the Wings of*

*the Mighty South Wind -*

*Ascend like a GOD*

*into Heaven*

SO BE IT

**AMEN**

# 00 *Epilogue* __The Invocation__

THE SOUTH WIND
(NINLIL, of
Evil Will)
breathes Plague
upon all peoples

- the Pestilence
She unleashes
on flesh
only
Holy
NINKARRAK
can appease - - -

If Her ill wind blow
again, then
Disease
so black
will
**attack**
all our nation
with fever will shake

In its wake *none may*
*sleep in peace* for
the blood shall
be d r a i n e d
from their
hearts till
they are
d e a d

*AND*

*NO*

*LIFE*

*WILL*

*BE*

*LEFT*

*O*
*WOE*
*TO*
*US!*

\*    \*    \*    \*    \*    \*

*Invoke*

*the Name*

*of* ADAPA - *for*

**His can Vanquish**

**this Sickness of Death**

*INVOKE*

*MY NAME*

**THEN YOU**

**SHALL BE**

**ALLOWED**

**TO LIVE**

"WHERE IS THE ONE WHO
CAN CLIMB UP TO HEAVEN? -
ONLY THE GODS LIVE FOREVER
WITH GLORIOUS SHAMASH

BUT AS FOR US MORTALS -
OUR DAYS ARE NUMBERED
- ALL THAT WE DO IS
BUT A BREATH
OF WIND"

# ADAPA's ASCENT

A Myth of Man & IMMORTALITY

# APPENDICES
# OF
# SUPPLEMENTARY
# MATERIAL

# ADAPA's ASCENT

# A. CHARACTER GLOSSARY

THE ENTIRE STORY OF *Adapa's Ascent* revolves around a very few characters. There are only seven players altogether, although just three are at the core of the drama: Adapa, Enki and Anu. As it may be helpful for some readers to have some basic knowledge of the characters of *Adapa's Ascent*, here are thumbnail sketches for each of them:

ADAPA - The central character of the drama is traditionally known as 'The Sage' and is a proto-type of the 'exorcist'. He finds himself - like a number of mythical heroes - halfway between Man and God, as his father is Enki, 'God of the Deep' (*i.e.* of the Sea). Adapa is offered the Food and Water of Immortality by Anu. However, due to Enki's misleading advice, he refuses it. Adapa is also written about as being a 'First Man' (like Adam) and may have been an early King, though - unlike Gilgamesh - there is no record of this.

ENKI - Also known as 'EA', this is one of the two chief Gods in *Adapa's Ascent*. He is known as the God of the Deep and also as the God of Wisdom. He is considered to be one of the Annunaki, an important group of deities who are offspring of Anu. He appears here as the father of

Adapa, giving him advice about what will happen when he is called to Heaven. He is the main God of the City of Eridu, where Adapa lives, and therefore the main focus of worship. He is seen as being the creator of Mankind itself and Adapa - His son - may represent Humanity as a whole.

ANU - Also known as AN, He is the Supreme God in the Sumero-Akkadian Worldview. He is the God of Heaven and the Father of the other Gods ('Annunaki'). While Anu rules the Firmament and Enki the Waters, Enlil - who does not appear in this narrative - rules the Earth. Anu is the most important character in this work apart from Adapa, as it is He who offers the Food and Water of Immortal Life to this human. Worship of Anu was centrally associated with Eanna's Temple in the City of Uruk. Anu was seen as "One Who Contains All The Universe".

NINLIL - This is an important Deity in *Adapa's Ascent* but only as an instigating factor of the main drama. Ninlil, also known as 'The Lady of the Wind', is the Goddess of the South Wind. She causes Adapa's boat to capsize while he is out fishing and he reacts to this with sheer anger and curses Her. It is by breaking Her wings with his words that the real drama commences, because

*Anu notices* that Ninlil is no longer blowing on the land. She is a daughter of Anu but there is debate about which Goddess is Her real mother.

DUMUZI - Also known as TAMMUZ, He is the God of Fertility and Vegetation. He is the companion of Gizzida, with whom we meet Him in *Adapa's Ascent,* in front of the Gates of Heaven. He most famously appears in the myth 'The Descent of Inanna', where He features as Inanna's husband. In that story He allows demons to drag Him down to hell in Inanna's place. Thus He is also known as being a God of the Underworld.

GIZZIDA - Also known as NINGIZZIDA and NINGISHZIDA, He is a companion God to Dumuzi, with whom He is destined to be "to All Eternity". He also is a God of Fertility and has been referred to as 'The Lord of the Tree of Life'. Dumuzi and Gizzida speak to Anu in Adapa's favor during the episode in Heaven. They do not have individual dialogue in this drama but share their words. Gizzida is also known as a God of Healing and Magic - a serpent with human head.

LLABRAT - He is the chief advisor to Anu and is described as 'Vizier' here. He sees to it that his Lord's commands are communicated to others.

" - WE NEED NEW MYTHS, BUT
WE NEED TO UNDERSTAND WE STAND
ON THE OLD MYTHS. THESE MUST BE
COMPLETELY UNDERSTOOD TO BE
ABLE TO CREATE NEW MYTHS "
JAMES G. FRAZER

# B. 'ADAPA's ASCENT'

## RECREATING AN ANCIENT CLASSIC

I AM NOT A SCHOLAR of Assyriology, professor of poetry or expert in philology. Why then - with none of these qualifications - have I decided to produce a translation of the Mesopotamian myth of Adapa? - Without being able to read Sumerian or Akkadian cuneiform, how have I been able to create a work that presents itself as a 'translation'? - At the outset, I wish to emphasize that I make no pretense of abilities that I do not possess and keenly sense a need to answer the questions above, as honestly and directly as possible, to explain *why* and *how* this poetic translation of '*Adapa's Ascent*' has come into existence.

## Discovering *Adapa's Ascent*

OVER A QUARTER OF A CENTURY has passed since I discovered a faded blue Penguin paperback - bearing the alluring title 'Before Philosophy' - in an antiquarian book cabinet at my childhood home in Leeds. It was hiding deep within a miscellany of dusty old tomes, paperback fiction and unevenly proportioned books on art theory, theology and cultural history. Being, even then, an avid reader of all volumes philosophical, the title instantly piqued my interest and I saved it from a precarious position under three creaking shelves of Walter Scott's 'Complete Works' in hardback. *How could I know what its impact would be?*

Turning to the contents page, I quickly discovered that this book was about the thought systems of Egypt, Mesopotamia and other ancient civilizations, prior to the emergence of speculative thought. Before flicking to some random pages, I was drawn in further by its original title: 'The Intellectual Adventure of Ancient Man'. I then realized that it was not by Henri Frankfort alone, but a compendium of academic essays by him and other experts on Assyriological Antiquity.

The only other thing I can remember clearly now, is that I turned to page 15 of the book (which I am looking at presently) and that the uncanny familiarity of the name 'Gilgamesh' caught my attention and prompted me to read what was written there: "*Gilgamesh and, in another myth, Adapa, are given a chance to gain eternal life simply by eating life as a substance*". Even though I felt strangely acquainted with the first of these two characters, I had never before heard the name of 'Adapa' and I wanted to know more. What I do remember from then, is that I instantly noticed the similarity of *his name* with 'Adam'. I continued to read: "*Adapa is offered bread and water of life when he enters heaven, but he refuses it on the instruction of the wily god Enki*".

"*Wow!*" I thought, what an amazing *plot-core*. — And from that moment on I was hooked by 'Adapa'. Only a few nuggets of information had been provided by Frankfort's study - but it was enough. This scene of Eternal Life *offered*, yet *turned down*, became firmly lodged in my cranium for over half a decade.

Without knowing any more details, the scenario had drawn me in *completely* and I was picturing imaginary dramas in my mind with the mythical 'Adapa'.

It is late 1999. I discover a tatty blue paperback in one of a dozen boxes of books I had transported to my apartment in London - years earlier. This time, I read it from cover to cover during a few dozen bus rides to and from the British Library, so irreversibly gripped am I by the 'Intellectual Adventure' of the Egyptians, Mesopotamians, Hittites and others. The first chapter in, I am already reminded of the tale of 'Adapa'. The name had indeed been niggling around in the back of my head and after being called to my mind again, I am determined to know more. New to the internet, on my very first iMac I launch Netscape Navigator and type '*Adapa + Eternal Life*' into Google. I wait for results, impatiently.

My eyes light up with the elation (of new knowledge) as I discover that half a dozen translations of 'Adapa' cuneiform tablets are in the top 10 hits. I am amazed at the helpfulness of technology and transfixed by each of the texts I read - though if you asked me to remember for sure which translations they were, I would not be able say. What I do recall clearly, is becoming aware that the Adapa narrative was based on a number of Akkadian fragments - also, that none of the texts which I found read anything like verse. Sure, they were presented somewhat like poetry, in lines of varying length, but there was no rhyme or rhythm, no musicality or lyricism in them. This was the first moment that I wondered - *could the myth of Adapa become poetry in English?*

Yet again, in spite of being mesmerized by the words that I read, I left 'Adapa' aside for another fifteen years! How could I do that? My only excuse is that life got complicated - cancer, autism, flood, disability, dementia, eviction, dire poverty - adversity clung to me like a friend and nothing worked out as we hoped it would. However, while living as a family of eight in a two-bed slum, I came across a copy of Shlomo Izre'el's study 'Adapa and the South Wind' on eBay. The moment my copy arrived and I opened it, I was drawn back into this ancient narrative just as if a whirlpool had sucked me down to Ea's watery depths.

This time, I was determined to find out everything I could about *Adapa,* and why this character had been pursuing me on and off for over twenty years. When meetings with certain people recur — *sometimes there is a good reason for it.* I felt that Adapa and I had unfinished business and so this time I was not prepared to let him out of my sight.

What did strike me, once I started to delve deeper, was how a version of the 'Adapa' narrative - in a complete form - appears all at once in about the 18th Century BCE. It changes over time, true, but it occurred to me (for a number of reasons given in my essay 'The Birth of Fiction') that it *could have* a longer narrative tradition than Gilgamesh, even if tablets of earlier date have not yet been unearthed.

# Researching *Adapa's Ascent*

FROM THE FIRST MOMENT that I came across 'Adapa', I was gripped by its core plot of a human being confronted with one of the most important decisions they could face— that of choosing (or refusing) Eternal Life. As I got more acquainted with English translations of the tablets, two ideas were colorfully swirling around in my head: Could this text not be expressed in the most captivating poetry? *and* - Do I feel that I am capable of accomplishing this myself?

I knew that one activity would be necessary first so as to answer these questions - I had to become fully acquainted with all of the source material, as well as most of the research that had been undertaken into the decipherment and interpretation of 'Adapa'. Izre'el's book was a guiding light in this regard as it was the first place that I found the actual images of the cuneiform tablets and the transcription of every single mark and symbol on them. In addition, its detailed bibliography sent me in the direction of dozens of other key researchers - and along with all the articles I could find on ResearchGate and Academia.edu, I quickly found myself immersed in what has evidently become one of the most vibrant and productive areas of Assyriological scholarship.

As anyone interested in the 'Adapa' narrative will quickly discover, the core sources of our knowledge are a mere baker's dozen of cuneiform tablets that range from the 18th to the 7th Century BCE.

There are, it is true, a number of additional fragments containing text pertaining to this story, but they mainly duplicate or do not add much extra to our knowledge of 'Adapa'. For the benefit of those who are not familiar with the sources, I want to mention them now as I will be referring back to them in the course of analyzing this poetic translation of 'Adapa'.

The stories of Adapa have been passed down to us on tablets from three different locations. The most *complete form* of the myth is known from the 'Amarna Tablet', as it was discovered in the archives of the Egyptian Pharaoh Amenophis IV (1377-1361 BCE) at Tell El-Amarna (Egypt) in 1887. It dates back to the 14th Century BCE and it is written in Akkadian cuneiform. It is also commonly referred to as 'Fragment B' and, for simplicity, I will usually refer to it as 'B' from this point onwards. The story of Adapa told here is the most continuous and undamaged record of the tale that exists, though it is missing elements that appear in later (and earlier) forms thereof - some of which we will consider later.

*Secondly*, there is a group of tablets that was found in the remains of the Library of King Ashurbanipal of Assyria (668-626 BCE) at Nineveh (Iraq). Tablets from his Royal Library were first excavated in 1849, though it was in 1876 that a key one of them was published by Assyriologist George Smith. They are known as Fragments 'A', 'A¹', 'C', 'D' and 'E'. They are - just like B - written in Akkadian cuneiform, although as you can see from the age of the library, they date from roughly seven hundred years *later* than the Amarna Tablet - *circa* the 7th Century BCE, known as the Assyrian period. Similar and different material is presented in these tablets, and they enable us to synthesize a more complete version of the story.

*Thirdly,* two versions of the Adapa story were found at Tell el-Haddad in about 1980, when an Old Babylonian library was discovered. What is significant about these tablets is that they are written in Sumerian cuneiform, dating back as far as 1760 BCE. They have recently been deciphered and transliterated into French by Prof. Antoine Cavigneaux (2014) and these two Sumerian versions are of great value in appreciating key elements of narrative which would remain constant throughout more than a millennium of being passed down. Also, these Sumerian tablets provide a *prequel* to the main narrative of 'Adapa', which is invaluable in understanding more deeply the significance of his personality within the drama. The 'Flood Prologue' helps us situate ourselves better in the context of a preceding train of events. No such long prologue is present in any of the other versions.

For most of the remainder of this essay, I am going to be discussing how I have used the material from these three sources in order to create this new version of 'Adapa', combining: (1) 14th Century BCE Akkadian tablets from Amarna; (2) 7th Century BCE Akkadian tablets from Nineveh; and (3) 18th Century BCE Sumerian tablets from Tell Haddad. The table on the following page clarifies this better.

## SOURCES of *Adapa's Ascent*:

| Source | Language | Contents |
|---|---|---|
| Fragment **A** Fragment **A**[1] (Nineveh) | Akkadian | *Documents Adapa leading his people, fishing for them; introductory words.* |
| Fragment **B** (Amarna) | Akkadian | *Full story of Adapa - from cursing the South Wind to his exile from Heaven.* |
| Fragment C (Nineveh) | Akkadian | *Passage regarding Anu's anger with Enki's deception.* |
| Fragment **D** (Nineveh) | Akkadian | *About Adapa being restored to Heaven and an Invocation.* |
| Fragment **E** (Nineveh) | Akkadian | *Extra passages on the South Wind.* |
| Fragments **S** [S[1]-S[6] relied upon here] (Tell Haddad) | Sumerian | *Complete Version of Adapa story with focus on the South Wind, plus lengthy 'Flood Prologue'.* |

When my interest in 'Adapa' was first ignited, I saw it as being a work in fragments - and one where a massive amount of speculation would be needed in order to fill the gaps and work out what the full story of it might be. However, after considering the materials over an extended period of time, it did appear to me that the sources may point toward the existence of a narrative that is longer than is standardly believed. Up till quite recently, the version represented by the Amarna Tablet (B) has been readily accepted as the core version of the 'Adapa' narrative. However, it is my belief that the Nineveh Fragments - as equally the two early Sumerian recensions - direct us to a *broader* narrative of 'Adapa' having existed, as well as having evolved over time. My intention has been to portray the most robust and complete version of 'Adapa' possible, from all the sources that are available.

Fragment B is the most complete single version of the 'Adapa' drama in Akkadian but, with the emergence of the Tell Haddad tablets of 'Adapa', we now have a Sumerian text whose core narrative is almost as 'whole' as the Tell Amarna version. Sure, the 'Flood Prologue' is seriously damaged in places, but the portions of the Tell Haddad texts that relate the story of Adapa cursing the South Wind and being brought to account for it — *these* are largely intact.

In my opinion, the fact that the Tell Amarna tablet tells one complete story about Adapa is not a reason to believe that it tells *all of the story of Adapa.* The 'Adapa' drama was passed down from generation to generation - whether in the form of a play, religious ritual or other type of enactment. This does not mean that a text that we discover - in one period of time or other - is going to represent what the majority of people learned about Adapa as part of their culture. After many years of reciting a story about the Flood, for instance, it may simply have become superfluous to include this element of the tale as it had become so well-known to everyone and was not necessary to relating the more specific narrative about the cursing of the South Wind by Adapa (and its consequences). Just because what I have called the 'Flood Prologue' is absent from the Amarna Tablet, does not mean it was absent from the minds of those who were reading that tablet — or writing it, for that matter.

I think the situation is similar to that of people reading the Bible and not needing to be reminded of the 'Adam' narrative in every one of the books subsequent to 'Genesis'. The story of the "First Man" becomes *common knowledge* - as it has been for several millennia now - and it is not essential to retread the plot points of that tale when telling the stories of Cain and Abel, Noah, Abraham or Moses. Everyone knows it well enough so that it can be left where it is in the back of everyone's minds - as an 'origins' prequel.

My aim has been to pay attention to all of the versions of the 'Adapa' legend that we have at our disposal and to ignore nothing. I believe that all of the texts that have come down to us are invaluable pieces of the 'Adapa' puzzle. I have created this new version of it because I believe that it may be possible to synthesize a complete text in English that does pay full credit to all the source materials available — one which benefits the modern reader as much as possible.

I think there *are* good reasons for being opposed to such a project - though I do not have time to discuss them here - though my core belief in the *potential value* of a synthesis of the Amarna, Nineveh and Tell Haddad versions of the text is what has driven me to produce the volume that you hold. It may be that Claude Lévi-Strauss is right when he says that all extant versions of a myth should be read in order to understand a myth as a whole. Whether or not this is true, *it is my belief* that in attempting to present the most complete version of the ʿAdapaʾ myth possible, the writer should derive the maximum advantage from each of the sources at their disposal.

Read together, I have found that I was able to understand each of the texts better in the light of each other. Fusing them together as I have - in this new version of ʿAdapaʾ - I have sought to make all of the elements introduced contribute to the whole: so that the parts shed new light on each other and so that the entirety glows with a greater overall luminosity.

The remainder of this essay is devoted to explaining how I have pieced this translation together from its constituent parts. In doing so, I was really blessed in being able to refer to the work of scores of translators and scholars who had studied the text before me, so I would like to discuss that briefly now.

# Translating *Adapa's Ascent*

IN APPROACHING THIS TASK, I was fortunate to be able to read and reflect on numerous translations of this text which have gone before. I have been able to review twenty translations of 'Adapa' that have preceded this one, and each has been of assistance in some way: George Smith's early translation of Fragment D; the translation of biblical scholar R.W. Rogers; translations in French (Talon), Italian (Picchioni), Spanish (Zamudio) and English (Foster; Dalley; Speiser); verse translation (Kilmer), transliteration from the cuneiform (Izre'el; Cavigneaux) and in continuous prose (Sandars) - to mention only a few. I have included further details on these translations in the 'Suggestions for Further Reading'.

At this point I would like to share a few of my observations on the translational work that has taken place and also to go some distance towards explaining - in exactly what sense - the work that I have produced can actually be called a 'translation'.

The core texts to which I have referred from the beginning to end of this process have been the editions of the cuneiform tablets published by Profs. Sergio Angelo Picchioni, Shlomo Izre'el and Antoine Cavigneaux. I have found these three guides the most instructive in their analysis of every symbol, mark and scar upon the group of tablets that are the basis of this translation. Without seeing the actual fragments and appreciating (due to their condition) the many areas of ambiguity and dispute in the interpretation of the symbols, it would not have been possible to strive toward an integral vision of 'Adapa'.

For those who are involved in Assyriological research today, it hardly needs mentioning that this is an immensely rich and active area of scholarship due to the massive quantity of cuneiform tablets that have been discovered over the past one hundred and fifty years, including a vast amount of tablets that were excavated almost forty years ago. Just in the case of 'Adapa' alone, there has been a grand harvest of articles, monographs and symposia dedicated to understanding the origins, authorship, meaning and purpose of this very significant narrative: Profs. J.M. Sasson, Piotr Michałowski, Sara J. Milstein, Giorgio Buccellati and N-E Andreason are just a *handful* of the key contributors to 'Adapa' research over the past few decades (without repeating the names of some of the vital translators and scholars on the preceding page).

As confessed at the outset of this essay, my own position is not that of a scholar or an academic professional. Over the past twenty years I have mainly been active as an author of poetry and philosophy, though throughout that time the thought has occurred to me that - *perhaps* - it would be possible for one to create a poetic version of the 'Adapa' narrative that would do some justice to the texts at the same time as drawing on the rich fields of research that have been sown and reaped over the past century and a half. It occurred to me as an *adventurous possibility*.

Previous to this I have only translated from French into English (Robbe-Grillet, Verlaine, de Lisle), German to English (Zweig, Kant) and Italian to English (Dante). However, I have been inspired to undertake the task of translating the 'Adapa' story into English - and to tread on the toes of Sumero-Akkadian scholars! - by the incredible example of the late Nancy Katharine Sandars. — Author of the popular Penguin volume, 'The Epic of Gilgamesh', Ms. Sandars is totally honest in admitting that hers was not a direct translation from the cuneiform, for: "*Such a translation would require a direct knowledge of the languages in which the various parts have survived - Sumerian, Akkadian and Hittite are the principle - and is a task which I am not competent to undertake*". Nonetheless, as most readers of that 60-page prose translation of the 'Gilgamesh' narrative will discover, it is an energetic, fresh and gripping presentation of the story which enabled this ancient text to reach a wider audience than it had before.

I mention this fact because I am acutely aware that - without being a cuneiform scholar - I cannot claim to have the first-hand experience of decipherment possessed by the majority of authors cited in the brief bibliography at the end of this book. Even though I have spent several years studying the actual tablets, transcriptions of their symbols, literal translations into English (and other languages) as well as much of the speculative literature that aids in interpretation - I cannot profess myself to be an expert in any way at all. *My purpose* is quite different to that of other translators who have approached this task — so I think it would be advisable for me to explain my standpoint and what has compelled me to proceed.

For all that has been gained in accuracy and understanding from detailed scrutiny of the tablets - and after so many varied and valuable translations have been produced - it still seemed to me that three things had not yet been accomplished, and I set out to do so with this new attempt at translating 'Adapa'.

*Firstly*, although I am not suggesting that all the existing translations are mere transliterations of the cuneiform transcriptions, none of them read to me like literature in its own right. In some instances, it is true, a degree of naturalness has been achieved in the language of the translations (Talon, Dalley, Sandars) but in most of them the language appears to me to be unnatural and stilted. This is understandable, given the ancient origins of the texts, but I have felt for a long time that it may be possible to express the text of 'Adapa' in a more fluid and literary way.

Above all, I do not believe that much success has been achieved in portraying this drama in *poetry*, for even though it has been taken up as a task of *versification* before, it has not been approached as a literary task — to set the entire work into poetic form. What I am aware of is that for all my deficiencies - above all, not being an expert in cuneiform - I have nonetheless approached this task from a different perspective, that of being a poet and not an academic. As the narrative of 'Adapa' is written in poetry, it is my opinion that it may be most fitting that it also be translated into poetry. I shall return to consider this in more detail in the following section of this essay.

*Secondly,* now that a far broader view of the 'Adapa' narrative has been gained, based on tablets bearing this story that span over one thousand years, it is possible *to attempt to synthesize* a version of this myth that takes all those diverse elements into account. Up to now, translations have largely been based on the Amarna Tablet - which makes sense, as it was for a long time the most complete recension - and it has been possible to grasp *part of* the drama of 'Adapa'. However, even though translations have been made from other tablets, containing much original material not found in the Amarna recension, up to this point no translation has brought together all of those assets into a single text. I believe that it is worth doing this and that errors made in doing so are likely to be outweighed by the positive benefits of beginning to appreciate the broader scope of the legend overall. This has been managed several times in the case of 'Gilgamesh', and I believe that doing so in the case of 'Adapa' could help us advance in understanding it.

*Thirdly* - as far as I can see - the 'Adapa' story has never been released as a single volume in a format for the *general public* to read. I think this has been a shame, for several generations of readers have not been in a position to enjoy this stimulating tale in the same way that its big brother ('Gilgamesh') has been appreciated. N.K. Sandars' translation of that work has been in print for over sixty years, and this has led to there being a general awareness of 'Gilgamesh' — whereas in spite of one and a half centuries of scholarly research and a large quantity of studies on 'Adapa', the public have not been able to witness what a breathtaking work this is, in its own right.

In my own opinion, 'Adapa' is a fundamental story — one in which its hero is involved in a *Drama of Immortality*. There is intrigue, deception, banishment and the use of magic - its plot, though miniature, containing all that an audience needs. In fact, with a mere trio of characters (Anu, Enki, Adapa), the ancient authors of this work have created a compelling story that reveals new perspectives each time that you read it. In spite of its slender size, it is a classic of world literature and it deserves a global audience.

In bringing this section to a close, I wish to emphasize that I make no claims to having composed a definitive translation of this opus. All that I have attempted to do has been to produce a version that is more approachable and accessible than those that have gone before and which, hopefully, will lead future generations of translators to produce one that is more artistic, more accurate and more readable.

What I wish to discuss now - in as much detail as a limited space permits - are the considerations and decisions that have been made during the composition of '*Adapa's Ascent* ' - **how it has been built**.

## Creating *Adapa's Ascent*

BEFORE EMBARKING ON a more intricate analysis of the *form* and *content* chosen for this version of 'Adapa', I would like to make a few general observations upon these two aspects we are about to discuss.

From the first time that I discovered 'Adapa', I knew that I wished to recreate it in a poetic format in the English language. It is the only language with which I am *truly* comfortable and I believe that in English it is capable of reaching the widest audience. Even before I was aware that the original texts were recorded (in cuneiform) as poetry, I was determined to convert 'Adapa' into English verse and not prose. However, when I came across S.A. Picchioni's *'Il Poemetto di Adapa'* in 2010, I realized - from the title of his book alone - that this work had been a poem to begin with, partly reassuring me of that decision.

When, years later, I became properly reacquainted with 'Adapa', I made a second key choice, one that would affect the content as opposed to the form of this work. I decided - in 2015 - that the version of 'Adapa' that I was going to create would base its narrative on *all available materials* so as to create a choate whole, even if some speculation were needed.

The only difference now - translating it in 2019 - is that since making those two decisions, my work was also affected by the 'Adapa' tablets found during the groundbreaking excavations near Tell Haddad. Those two Sumerian texts - mentioned briefly in the previous section - have transformed the landscape of 'Adapa' scholarship, giving us a broader view of what narrative elements have changed (and which stayed the same) over a period in excess of a thousand years.

Even though it has taken me a long time to reach this point (and I have been distracted from this translation in all ways imaginable) my original intentions have remained the same. My vision was to recreate an integral version of the Adapa narrative - relying on all fragments existing - and for this to be expressed in poetry throughout. The difference is that while I had a vague plan in my head to create a version of 'Adapa' in verse at the very start of my career in poetry - when I had only released 'In a Short Space of Time' (1999) - I am now finally completing this work after two decades of writing works of poetry. Although - on the one hand - I wish that it had been the first and not one of my last volumes of poetry, at the same time I am glad that I have been practising this art for two decades, so that this work benefits from years of practice and is not the début of a dilettante.

The truth is that this has been the most difficult poetic work I have ever written. For it has not been an issue of pleasing myself, but of meeting many other standards - not the least of which has been my sincere desire to do justice to the text itself and its original authors, however many they may be. I have also been conscious - throughout the creative process - of how widely I may be diverging from what is expected (and accepted) as a translation of the 'Adapa' texts.

## REGARDING **FORM**

IT IS NOT ENTIRELY POSSIBLE to extricate issues of form and content from each other as regards the composition of this translation - however, I will do my best to discuss these two topics in turn, separately.

The only choice that I have mentioned up to this point, regarding *form*, is that I decided to translate the 'Adapa' narrative into English verse as opposed to prose. On the one hand, I did find consensus among scholars that the 'Adapa' fragments are written in poetic formats (Dietrich; Molino & Tamine; Izre'el) and in regards to the Amarna version of the text, for example, the last-named author writes that it: "*abounds in poetic devices*" and was "*composed by a poet who had an intimate knowledge of contemporary Babylonian language*". If this were not enough, he goes on to remark that it "*can be regarded as a piece of poetry because it applies metrical-rhythmic organization to its linguistic organization*" and "*includes, in addition to metrical organization and poetic language, salient features of poetry, such as alliteration and other sound phenomena, repetition and parallelism*". — Professor Izre'el's depth of poetic analysis is the most detailed yet among 'Adapa' scholars and he has detected all of the poetic phenomena mentioned as well as the usage of successive lines of decreasing length, onomatopoeia and possible marking of metrical/poetic units with black/red points on the tablets. Thus, many factors confirm the *poetry* of 'Adapa'.

However, just because recensions of the work have been identified as poetry *does not mean* that it is a foregone conclusion that the best way of translating it is into poetry in another language. Looking at the majority of translations made of the 'Adapa' narrative heretofore, they have been translations into prose - though it is true that the French, Spanish and Italian renditions of the text are noticeably more poetic due to the musical qualities of these languages.

Taking the example, yet again, of 'Gilgamesh', even though this has long been known to be a poetic work, the most popular version of it (Sandars, 1960) is set in prose. The earliest known form of the work is a collection of five poems written in Sumerian and, looking at the most complete version of 'Gilgamesh' (the 'Ninevite Recension'), this is composed of twelve songs (or 'cantos') of about three hundred lines each, inscribed on individual tablets. For the most part, it is in poetry that has four beats per line, although a Babylonian version exists that has two beats per line. All this, however, did not mean that 'Gilgamesh' *had to be translated into poetry*. As Sandars has proven, prose is able to be an effective translation choice even when an original work has been composed in poetry.

Another pertinent example would be the E. V. Rieu translation of Homer's 'Odyssey' epic, for even though the original was, of course, written in Greek verse, the Penguin editor's decision to compose his version in English prose was both effective and successful — proven by the fact it is still in print today.

My stance is that it is both a translational and artistic decision to convert a piece of writing from one form into another. It is not erroneous to translate a piece of poetry into prose, or *vice versa*. Translation is - in one sense - an art, and as with most arts this involves making bold decisions. What matters most is whether the translator - as an artist with words in their own right - is up to the task that they have set themselves and capable of casting their new version of the work being translated into the format chosen.

In the case of Sandars, I do believe that her translations of 'Gilgamesh' (1960) and 'Adapa' (1970) are both effectual in achieving her goal of relating their stories in fluid and natural prose. Having chosen prose as the format, it is not possible to judge her version of 'Gilgamesh' as being inferior, for example, to that of Prof. Andrew George, *just because* it is not set in poetry. However, it *does* need judging on the inherent qualities of her prose and on the fidelity with which the translation expresses the source texts from which it is derived - and upon these criteria the scholars and critics may harbor differing opinions.

I do not have the time or ability to analyze the varying poetic formats and devices used in the different 'Adapa' tablets. These change significantly from the early Sumerian version through to the Amarna recension, and finally in the Ninevite fragments. However, you need only take a glance at any out of a dozen passages to see the most obvious poetic musicality of the language utilized by their authors.

Take, for instance, lines 5-6 of Fragment A[1] (without translating them here) which read, once transcribed:

*balu gissi kannima*
*balu gis gi mussima*

You do not need to be a student of poetry or scholar in Assyriology to appreciate the sheer sonority of these lines. Both of them have seven syllables and the elements of repetition, rhyme and soundplay are so conspicuous that no-one would fail to notice.

Take, as one more example, lines 64-65 of B, where Adapa is being brought a garment and oil:

*lubaru ilqunissumna ittalbas*
*samna ilqunissumna ittapsis*

The repetition and musicality of the language is so apparent on reading it out loud that there can be no doubt - on the basis of these examples, at least - that this work has been framed in poetry and not prose.

A few words are in order, at this point, on **how** I have chosen to depict 'Adapa' in verse. I have taken time to consider whether to try and accurately replicate the metrical patterns, rhythm and rhyme (plus other devices) as and when they appear in the original cuneiform of the narrative. However, with English being such a hugely different language from Sumerian and Akkadian, my decision has been to recreate 'Adapa' in poetic forms that feel natural to me in English and that allow me to express its narrative in my own way. It would be possible, I believe, for someone to accomplish a great translation of this work into one of the Semitic languages, due to their greater similarity with Akkadian — however, in my own case (as I predominantly write poetry in the English language) I have not attempted to copy any types of wordplay that I became aware of in the originals. All similarities of a linguistic nature are more or less accidental as I have not - in any place - been able to emulate the original authors in any manner.

I do not believe that it would be worthwhile for me to analyze or attempt to justify the forms of poetry and verbal play that I have exercised in the forty-four pages of this 'Adapa' translation. I have used all of the tools and techniques at my disposal - those I felt were appropriate to the task. With the benefit of all the advancements in 'Adapa' scholarship over more than 150 years, I have done my utmost to express *in my own language* what I believe is expressed - albeit in very different manner and format - within the originals. My poetry is as different from the poetry of the core texts as English poetry and English prose are different from each other.

What I will also say, is that I have not made a contrived effort to frame the 'Adapa' tale in any single poetic form (iambic pentameter, alexandrines, couplets, quatrains, Kalevalan meter *inter alia*) but I have considered the substance of each stage of its drama in an individual fashion and I have used the wordplay that seemed most fitting to each of its parts. Somehow, my aim has been to forge a middle path between what is communicated in the originals - in Sumerian and Akkadian - and how I believe contemporary readers may be most capable of appreciating and understanding the text in Modern English. My wish has been to strike a perfect balance, but only readers can determine if I have succeeded in doing so. I am still too close to the task I have completed to be able to view it with the requisite level of objectivity. In fact, it may be that I am never able to appraise my own work.

The core aim of the forms and language that I have utilized in *Adapa's Ascent,* has been to bring its drama before the reader's imagination in the most clear and vivid fashion possible. I have asked myself - in the case of each verse and section of the poem - how can I express the story on the page in a way that best enables it to speak to the contemporary reader?

In some cases, rhyme has been the apposite choice, on other occasions alliteration or play with the meter of successive lines. Whatever seemed *most natural* has been the determining factor in the majority of my choices - though I would confidently say that, throughout this version of 'Adapa', rhythm has been the binding thread. In that regard, I have always aimed to discover the *most natural rhythm* with which to communicate the story in words. I have tried not to force any of the verses into uncomfortable contortions or unwieldy constructions. What I have composed may make sense when read in one's head, but in order to take it in, as it has been intended, I think that the words really need to be read aloud.

The only other feature of this version which I wish to discuss at this point - as it also relates to form - is the manner in which I have subdivided the work in a way that has not been done before. Instead of presenting *Adapa's Ascent* as a continuous poem, I have opted to separate the work into a series of chapters, preceded by a short prologue and followed by an epilogue. The content of these sections, I will shortly describe, but I wish to justify my decision to partition the work in this way, before turning to issues that relate to content in the following subsection.

As will become clear shortly, through a section-by-section analysis of *Adapa's Ascent* (in which I will give my explanations for *what* I have included, in *which sequence*, and *why*), this version has played with the order of text to an extent which I believe is permissible in order to reach the modern English reader with an optimum level of comprehensibility.

The medium of most familiarity to the reader of today, is *the novel*. This is the key format of fiction writing that is consumed by the general public, so it is not, in my belief, amiss to present the current work in a way which conforms - at least to a minimal extent - with the format of the novel. This is one reason why the partitioning of *Adapa's Ascent* makes it easier for the work to be read. 'Chapters' are a "way in" for regular readers and by providing them with these structural signposts, they are more readily able to get a grasp on a work which is - when represented as it is on the extant tablets - virtually impenetrable.

Nor do I think that the introduction of chapter divisions - where not previously existing - is only of help in works of poetry or fiction. In editing a new edition of F.W.J. von Schelling's 'Philosophical Investigations into the Nature of Human Freedom', I introduced a fresh division of the book into chapters, which - although this varied from how the author had *originally presented* it - helped to *re-present* to the reader the contents of that work in a more digestible way. The author's treatment of topics was clarified and the sequence of his reasoning was made plainer.

One of the reasons why the 1960 'Epic of Gilgamesh' (from *Penguin Books*) worked so well - and appealed to a large public - was because its translator presented the work, not according to a twelve-tablet structure based on the Ninevite recension, but in an eight-chapter format (including a prologue), each of whose titles indicated clearly what their content was. Even though *Adapa's Ascent* is a poetic work, that does not mean that it is unadaptable to the kind of chapter format that is more typical of fiction works.

I can understand why purists could object to experimenting with the division and order of a work that has an established history and which has become fixed in a particular edition - for example, the 'Amarna recension', in the case of Adapa - but looking at the history of works as they are published, how different are the various publishing houses' editions of the same author's work? - Is it not inevitable that the same can happen in the history of this piece? -

Looking at Homer's 'Odyssey' and the 'Epic of Gilga-mesh' as examples — how many different editions and translations have they gone through, some barely recognizable as the same work, so different are their vocabularies and formats and overall presentation?

There are *good reasons* for editions of 'Adapa' that include all of the tablets and the fragments of cuneiform - presenting them as photographs, as diagrams, as transcripts, as transliterations *etc.* These are, however, of most use to the scholarly community and still leave the fiction work of 'Adapa' at a great distance from the general reader, remaining to them inaccessible. It is my *view* - already expressed at an earlier point in this essay - that the drama of 'Adapa' has been kept away from the general public for too long and it is my *hope* that this new version (flawed and error-ridden though it be) may be one route via which a new age of readers becomes aware of 'Adapa'.

Being truthful about my own experience of the 'Adapa' narrative - I found this story impossible to make sense of in every one of the translations that I was able to lay my hands on. One of the reasons that I decided to spend time with this work was precisely because I wanted to work out what it was all about. Once I had attained a moderately better understanding of the plot and its potential meanings, I became committed to ensuring that others who approached this work - who are unable to access it in its original languages - would be more easily capable of comprehending that work *without so much effort.*

## REGARDING **CONTENT**

THE QUESTION OF WHAT is to be included and what is to be omitted, has been the most important one to address in the composition of this new translation of the ʿAdapaʾ myth. I tried to make common-sense decisions in doing so but after spending such a long time in isolation with the texts it is possible that some of the decisions I have made will not make as much sense to others as they do to me. Before proceeding to a section-by-section analysis of this translation, I would like to say a few words about some more general issues that I have had to contend with during composition - and some of the key considerations that affected the way in which I have gradually progressed to an endpoint that I could deem acceptable.

In the earlier section, ʿResearching Adapaʾ, I reviewed what are the most important known sources of the ʿAdapaʾ narrative - the core source texts upon which this translation is based. Please refer back to the table on p.60 for an ʿat-a-glanceʾ reminder of the fundamental materials upon which I have depended.

Several paths to proceed along presented themselves to me and it took a lot of deliberation before I was able to definitively choose which I should follow.

The *first approach* that I had as an option, was that of basing this translation on the oldest of the existing versions of the ʿAdapaʾ narrative (in Sumerian), that is, on either or both of the recensions of ʿAdapaʾ that were found near Tell el-Haddad *c.*1980.

Such a translation would have paid full attention to the cuneiform tablets from this location only (which date back almost 3800 years), while ignoring all later appearances of the drama in the Akkadian language.

This was a viable option and one which might have generated a valuable end result. Prof. Cavigneaux's French transliteration of the cuneiform text would have served as primary guidance as well as the output of a number of scholars whose works - in recent years - have delved deeper into the meaning and purpose of the original Sumerian texts. However, one of the downsides of making those early versions the subject of any poetic translation into English, is that there are such significant gaps in the texts that any attempt at accurately translating them now would be highly prone to error. We are also at a disadvantage with those texts due to the juvenile status of research into them, though additional years of analysis may provide more key results. Furthermore, there are not - as is the case with the Amarna Tablet - numerous translations from different scholars' perspectives, so that varying interpretations of the cuneiform symbols can be proposed, debated about and contemplated.

At this stage, it is only too likely that all attempts at accuracy will be doomed to plunge into pits of error, as I undoubtedly have done with my 'Translation Sketch of a Sumerian Text' (*qv.* Appendix D).

Moving on to a *second alternative* - there was the option of producing a poetic translation of the Amarna Tablet alone. That, to be fair, is a far more feasible task as there has been a veritable outpouring of scholarly papers on this source and there already exists almost a score of translations of this recension of the 'Adapa' narrative alone. Being a more mature text (1400 BCE) may also be considered a benefit, as well as the fact that Akkadian - in which this version is written - is better understood than Sumerian.

Lastly - and perhaps most significantly - this version of the 'Adapa' narrative is the single most complete and least damaged source of the story in existence. This means that it is possible to produce a poem that has maturity and continuity at the same time - which does seems like an attractive option to select. One compelling argument against producing a poetic translation of this version alone, is precisely that *so many attempts have already been made*.

Nonetheless, one response to this could be that, of those translations produced up to now, only a few of them have made any effort to set 'Adapa' in *verse* and none of those poetic endeavors have been produced by a poet. The translations that have attempted to be poetic thusfar seem more like 'academic versification' than bona fide poetry. The possibility of translating the Amarna tablet *solely*, was one that was considered as a real alternative for several of the reasons above.

The '*third alternative*' was that of producing a complete translation of 'Adapa' from the youngest cuneiform tablets in Akkadian - the Nineveh Fragments (*c.* 700 BCE) - which was simply not an eligible option because, even though these source texts contain much valuable material, they do not provide us with a single, cohesive narrative of the 'Adapa' drama. We find duplicates of scenes present in both the Tell Haddad and Amarna recensions, as well as scenes that are absent from both of those. But when it comes to producing a translation based on these fragments alone, it is in no way viable. It is true that - like the Amarna Tablet - they have been keenly researched and do provide key missing pieces of the drama, but a key disadvantage is that they are in a worse condition (*e.g.* Fragments C and D) and therefore their interpretation requires a great deal more speculation.

Those are three options, at any rate - the last of which is ruled out due to the Nineveh texts not providing a complete plot. On further consideration, however, I do believe that there are three more options available. Let me quickly state what these are and then move onwards to justify the choice that I made out of the half a dozen that were on offer.

A realistic *fourth option* - and one which has actually been broached to a degree by some translators of the cuneiform texts into prose - would be to create a unified poetic version of the 'Adapa' narrative that is based on both the Amarna Tablet and the Nineveh Fragments. The positive advantages of this are that: (a) where two versions of the same episode appear in separate recensions, it is possible to be more certain of the text by relying on them both; where there is damage or ambiguity to one tablet or fragment, it is possible to refer to a second version for confirmation of what the symbols are; and (b) where the Nineveh Fragments provide additional episodes or material that is not present in the Amarna recension, these can be included in this type of merged version at the most appropriate points. In fact, it could also be claimed that: (c) it is a very *plausible* choice because both of the source texts are in Akkadian; and that (d) the already complete, combined-research into the Amarna Tablet and Nineveh Fragments provides maximum grounding for the translation on properly investigated sources. — I can agree with the above, and I believe it makes good sense to add additional sections to a translation by including material from a later period (especially when there are so few sources available), in this case, the text of the 7th Century BCE updating the 14th Century BCE text to a more modern Akkadian vision. Perhaps later recensions of 'Adapa' will be discovered in due course - that will add to the materials - but in my case, with this book, the above alternative was the one I was going to opt for, before I became aware of the Tell Haddad sources.

There is a *fifth choice* - which became possible since the discovery of those new and earliest sources - to create a poetic translation based on *all those texts* plus the Amarna Tablet also. Strong arguments can be offered in support of this choice, including: (a) the recensions from these two periods provide complete versions of the story and in fact mirror each other in key ways, so that they are eminently congruent with one another as source texts; (b) having a version of 'Adapa' based on two different languages within the key source texts (Sumerian and Akkadian) makes the linguistic basis of such a translation broader - and some might also say *firmer* - as the final result possesses dual linguistic lineage; and (c) the Tell Haddad recensions of the narrative include the substantial 'Flood Prologue' that sets the scene for the drama that follows in a way that is absent from the later versions. It seems a pity to lose all that additional narrative, which must be left to one side if the Tell Haddad recensions are ignored.

However, even though the above are good reasons for basing a translation on *complete versions* of the text only, the question arose in my mind: Why *forfeit* all the advantages provided by the Nineveh Fragments - the resolution of textual ambiguities, presence of additional episodes, linguistic variations and so forth, *when all this could also flow into the accuracy and dynamics of the text being created?* — These, and other considerations discussed below, were what led me in the direction of 'omni-inclusivity' in terms of my attitude to the sources to be relied upon.

The *sixth* and *final approach* that I have been able to identify - and the one which I felt most inclined to proceed with - was that of creating a translation of the 'Adapa' narrative based on the Tell Haddad *and*

Amarna recensions *as well as* the Nineveh Fragments. After spending an appreciable amount of time considering all of the options, this is the one that I chose.

The main reasons for making that decision were: (a) as we are now so fortunate to possess source material from *three separate periods*, it seems like a waste not to take full advantage of **all** *the material*; (b) one of the most reassuring results, based on surveying the versions from these three periods, is that a significant quantity of similar episodes are testified to by these texts as a group - and we can have a greater degree of certainty about those episodes testified to by multiple sources than those which only appear in one source; and also (c) as in the case of the fourth alternative mentioned above - that of doing a combined translation of the Amarna Tablet and the Nineveh Fragments - the reasoning that the extra episodes in the latter (*e.g.* Adapa's Return to Heaven) add to the substance of the work is also true of the Tell Haddad texts. Being able to *bear in mind* the 'Flood Prologue' during composition - even if not including it - does have an impact on the translation. Ignoring those texts would lead to a different result.

A few words on *general approach* and *modus operandi* during creation of this work are in order now. — That it was a totally unique task to face and one through which I could not plot my path beforehand, is defintely true to say. Having now completed the process of grappling with source materials from three non-contiguous time periods, I have reached a number of general conclusions that I wish to share.

I do feel that the Amarna Tablet provides us with the *key* to working out the vital order of events in the story; also, that it assists a great deal in our trying to determine the optimum placement of extra episodes derived from other sources. Comparing the Amarna version with the texts from Tell Haddad, it seems to me that in the intervening period - of about seven hundred years - there occurred maturation and sharpening of the narrative and thematic elements.

Amid all else that is going on during the plot, I sense the overarching powers of '*Destiny*' in that Akkadian version, whereas this theme only appears to be nascent and undeveloped in the Sumerian one. It increasingly feels to me as if the essential core of the story is that *Mortals* and *Gods have different lives and different destinies* - and that for a human being to act in a manner that the Gods do, is unbecoming of mortals, not to be encouraged in any way.

Deceiving his son, Adapa - if that is actually what Enki is aiming for with his advice to Adapa that he reject what he is given, thereby forfeiting Eternal Life offered him by Anu - may fit in with ensuring that Adapa's Destiny *remain what it should be*. It is not the Destiny of a human being to become a God — Immortality is a purely divine attribute, so to accept Eternal Life from a God would be *against* Destiny.

It is true that there are passing references to 'Destiny' over the course of the Sumerian version, but this theme only gained greater weight by the time of the Akkadian versions, especially by the 7th Century.

In spite of their being situated at a more infantile stage in the development of 'Adapa', the Tell Haddad texts do provide a few pointers to comprehending this work as a whole, in a more diverse way. Setting out clearly that Adapa was a 'First Man' and partly responsible - in collaboration with the Gods - for reëstablishing humankind on Earth, is one particularly important element of the Sumerian sources. Another feature that genuinely stands out, is how the focus on characters is differently emphasized - where in the Amarna Tablet it is Adapa who is the primary character of the drama, in the early Sumerian versions Enki appears to receive an equal amount of focus to Adapa, and the South Wind gets a larger degree of attention. In the Akkadian tablets, the South Wind appears only as a minor character — crucial, because her being cursed by Adapa gets Anu's attention, yet she is not given any substantial 'stage time'. There, she is just an instigating factor, not a significant actor.

In terms of the balance of attention between Adapa and Enki, I find it particularly noteworthy that the Sumerian version closes with an incantation - just like in the Nineveh Fragments - yet in that version the prayer is made in Ea's name, not Adapa's. *When did this shift take place?* It will be very interesting to see what any intervening tablets reveal.

Although there is *this* difference in terms of whom an invocation is made to, the earliest and most recent versions of 'Adapa' both appear congruent in their portrayal of the power of words and the 'magic' that they are capable of bringing about. — There has been a particular focus, in recent years, on Adapa's being the original 'Exorcist', as numerous documents have been found in which the rites of exorcism are being invoked in Adapa's name (*qv.* Amar Annus's study 'The Overturned Boat'). It appears that during the process of doing an exorcism, the Sumerians, Akkadians and Babylonians believed that the one fulfilling this role *did actually become Adapa* for the duration of that rite. It is telling that some Tell Haddad tablets of 'Adapa' were found in the library of an exorcist (Cavigneaux). On this, there is much to learn from Prof. Milstein, who explores 'the "magic" of Adapa' in her article of that name.

On the level of a footnote, I do not see it as significant that the 'Invocation' is absent from the Amarna tablet. As a teaching text, I do not believe that it was essential for it to include *all* the 'Adapa' text or episodes. Also, it is possible that the prayer was so well-known by that time, that it was not necessary to include it at the end of the text. I have proposed, earlier in this essay, that the 'Flood Prologue' could have been omitted from some recensions of 'Adapa' because its tale was so well-known that it no longer had to be included. I think it is possible that the invocation was absent from some editions for the same reason - while the key purpose of the narrative as a whole may still have been to explain the magical power of Adapa - how merely his name can cure.

As far as the primary translation featured in this book is concerned ('*Adapa's Ascent*'), I chose not to include a lengthier prologue by relying on material from the Sumerian versions, as I felt that by adding it to the narrative, this might well unbalance the rest of the plot; also, because there are so many lacunæ in those texts, my wish was to minimize the presence of speculative passages, not to increase this. However, because I do think that both the 'Flood Prologue' and Sumerian recensions are of real merit, I have done my best to create a 'Translation Sketch' of those earlier versions which may be of interest to some readers — included as Appendix 4 (pp.169-187).

One other element of my approach to this translation that will be noticeable, is the degree to which I wholeheartedly integrate episodes from the Nineveh Fragments into it. I find that the passages from that recension (incomplete though it be) are massively invigorating in terms of the new aspects of Adapa and his myth that they reveal. Not only are the passages about Adapa's re-admission to the Heavens of the highest interest, but equally the passages where Adapa is introduced performing his duties for Enki - as also one where Anu appears to be taking issue with how Enki has counselled Adapa to behave. Without the inclusion of all passages salvaged from the Nineveh Fragments, this translation would be of a very different nature - and in my opinion, inferior.

What does appear truly remarkable to me is that the Amarna recension appears to pick up exactly where Fragment A (Nineveh) leaves off. Just after the latter tablet has told us of the duties fulfilled by Adapa for Enki, the former tablet tells us of how he set sail for his divine father, so as to catch carp for him.

What lingers in the back of my mind - as I look over all of the versions of this legend - is that there might well be far superior sources of 'Adapa': more mature, more refined, more complete. But the reality is that we simply do not know of them yet. Will other tablets be found of 'Adapa'? *Of course - maybe - never* — no-one knows the answer. For now, all we can do is to make best use of the materials at hand. Whether my choice, to synthesize an integral text from the sum of all the 'Adapa' sources, has been the correct one, is not a question that I feel capable of answering at this time. It was a choice that I arrived at based on feelings and intuition, moreso than on reasoning and logic. What I have learnt, while attempting to spend an equal amount of time with each of the source texts, is that each of them assists us in understanding the others better. Though there are portions missing, significant damage to those that have survived, and key differences between them, by viewing all sources as pieces of one narrative, the vision of a unified whole can commence to materialize in one's mind. I believe that the dramatic unity of the 'Adapa' narrative can best be appreciated by endeavoring to assemble all the parts in a way that they naturally harmonize. —

# Composing _Adapa's Ascent_

I HOPE THAT the preceding pages have managed to lay bare my general approach to the writing of this translation. It is now time to move on to a more detailed analysis of its contents in a section-by-section manner. Here I shall get down to the "nuts and bolts" of what happened in the writing process and I will reveal how the whole has been constructed from its component parts, just as if we were dismantling an engine so as to see how the motor functions inside.

I do not think that a translation is merely the result of one or more general decisions being taken — rather, that it is composed of a large number of smaller choices being made regarding every individual aspect of the text: linguistic, structural, stylistic _et cetera_.

This has happened in the instance of _Adapa's Ascent_ - for many long days have been spent deliberating on what some could see as merely _minor issues_. When, for example, there are half a dozen nuances of meaning in the cuneiform original and it is a matter of making the best decision in the context of the story as a whole, this is when time is valuably spent.

In order to arrive at the final version as you find it here, I have often changed my mind on wording used in a passage as many as a score of times before I was satisfied that it was the best that I could reach. That being said, just because I had to make final decisions regarding every symbol and line, does not mean that I am satisfied with this translation to the extent that I can announce: "nothing needs changing". 'Perfectionism' never figured in my aims, and I am acutely aware that with the accelerating speed of 'Adapa' scholarship, it is ever more likely that new discoveries and interpretative progress will eradicate many speculative conclusions. Some of my guesswork may be proven to be downright wrong - perhaps in some areas new texts will leave my renditions open to debate, though it is even possible that some of my wilder postulations could be vindicated in future!

In spite of my feeling that this work would never come to a close, I did - after countless interruptions and delays - finally arrive at an end-point to this translation. I do not feel capable of accomplishing any more, and even though I know it will undoubtedly soon be supplanted by more poetic, better-researched and more complete versions of 'Adapa', this is all that I can achieve, so I lay down my pen.

Though it may only interest a small audience of readers, those who are curious or confused about the existence (or inclusion) of certain passages will find that the following forty plus pages of this essay do attempt to explain a step-by-step decision-making process that has gone into the creation of this poem. It is not a detailed exegesis of the texts with beat-by-beat justification of each line of text composed - that would be futile, and I believe, ultimately impossible.

The composer of poetry can go some distance in elucidating the manner in which she or he has written their verse, down to a certain level of detail.

However, I do not believe it is incumbent on a poet to dissect and argue in favor of every single decision that they have made. That is not say that an explanation of how a work has been put together - in more general terms - cannot be of interest to some. But the ideal kind of analysis - which would include cross-references to academic literature, comparison with variant wordings of previous translations, as well as the inner reasoning of all key decisions that have been made - this, unfortunately, I am unable to provide here, to that standard. In the miniature commentary that follows, I am only able to give a small glimpse into selected areas. In the case of each section of *Adapa's Ascent*, I provide the following details (except where irrelevant) as briefly as possible:

- *the name of the chapter and the pages it occupies;*

- *what happens within that section (the 'action') summarized in as few sentences as are required;*

- *where the section of text has come from - specifying the Tablet/Fragment it is from and the line numbers that have been translated by the text;*

- *remarks about the positioning of the chapter in this version and how it compares with the originals;*

- *in those instances where ambiguity exists and an interpretative decision has been made, the reasoning behind the choice made is explained in brief;  plus*

- *where the passage has a more speculative basis, further reasoning is given regarding its appearance.*

## A NOTE ON THE **TITLE** AND **PERIPHERAL TEXT**

BEFORE ADVANCING into this cursory exegesis of the complete text of *Adapa's Ascent*, a few words need to be said on the title given to this translation, as well as about some elements of peripheral text that feature within this version. This will not hold us up for long but as a title is so fundamental to any publication, it is worthwhile discussing how the title of the present work was arrived at, and with what reasons.

### The Title - 'Adapa's Ascent'

It has been noted by several key authorities (Izre'el; Rollig *et alia*) that a possible title to the 'Adapa' narrative is referred to in the 'Catalogue of the Cuneiform Tablets in the Kouyunjik Collection of the British Museum' (Bézold). It appears that there is a brief fragment of text that runs: "*a-da-pà a-na qé-reb* AN [*-el* ]" which translates into English as '*Adapa into Heaven*', which is very appropriate.

Adapa's journey to Heaven is *central* to the whole of the narrative — for he journeys to Heaven to see the supreme God, Anu, and after being relegated to earth he returns to Heaven in passages that have reached us from Nineveh. What I have done is to change this rather awkward and inchoate phrase (at least as it reads in English) into a simple title that includes two substantives conjoined by a possessive: '<u>Adapa's Ascent</u>'. It thus became the title of this book - both because I believe it is in alignment with the *potential title* that has been unearthed and also because it relevantly refers to the work's core plot.

It is not odd for a work to be set in writing yet to be without a title, in earlier periods of literature. 'Gilgamesh', as a literary opus, was long known by its first line "He who saw the Deep", but it did not have a title as such and was probably just referred to as 'The Gilgamesh Poem' in a similar way that the 'Iliad' just means 'Poem of Ilion' (*Ilion* being the ancient name for Troy). Moving forwards as far as the putatively English epic 'Beowulf', completed around 1000 CE, this does not have any title in the first and original 'Nowell Codex' - yet that is of little concern. The need for titles is not absolute but it just makes it easier to refer to an opus. In my opinion, it also serves the dual purpose of being able to express - in the fewest words possible - what that work is about.

A few words of explanation are needed as this translation of 'Adapa' does not straight away commence with the first lines of the narrative as they appear in the Amarna Tablet - to which we will turn next. Instead, I have opened this version with two verses which are not based on any of the core sources listed on p.60. The opening lines to this translation are: "*ADAPA, Born of the Sea, O So Wise One*" — then continuing in a similar vein. What I have opted to do is to combine the most common epithets about Adapa with the etymological bases of the two names 'Adapa' and 'Oannes' in order to construct what is simply a two-verse, thumbnail sketch of the hero.

## Opening Passage

I am not going to give a line-by-line break-down of this alternative opening (pp.0-1) but the source materials are not hard to find. In Akkadian lexical texts it is easy enough to discover that the word 'adapu' can mean *wise* — which obviously suits our hero Adapa, who became widely known as 'The Sage'. There is also perhaps some sound support for the line "Born of the Sea", as the Sumerian equivalent of 'adapu' is 'ù.tu.a.ab.ba' meaning "born in the sea".

Two more sources of value in creating the opening verses have been: (a) the alternate name for Adapa, '*Uan*' (Sumerian), which is intriguing be-cause it contains an implicit indication of Heaven due to the inclusion of the letters 'An' (which mean 'Heaven'); (b) an extract from a bilingual Sumero-Akkadian account of the First Sages, cited in Erica Reiner's article 'The Etiological Myth of the Seven Sages'. There she translates two lines which quite possibly refer to Adapa, reading: "*the purification priest of Eridu [...] who ascended to heaven*".

Furthermore, the reader may find it helpful to refer to an account of Adapa recorded by Greco-Babylonian historian Berossus (3rd Century BCE) wherein he describes 'Oannes' [Adapa] as a half-man/half-fish who: "*appeared from the Erythrean Sea in a place adjacent to Babylonia*".

Beyond that, I make no excuses for this open-ing passage that I have synthesized from a group of disparate materials. Although external to the text proper, I believe it sets the tone in terms of introducing Adapa with metaphors and epithets that Mesopotamians would have been familiar with at the time.

## Closing Passage

The second peripheral element added to this version of 'Adapa' - not based upon any of the core sources - is to be found on the final page (p.43), where I have created two verses directly after the 'incantation' in which Adapa's name is explicitly exhorted at the end as a means of averting evil: above all, illness. In the 'Utukku Lemnutu Incantations' (Babylonian) the protagonist of our drama describes himself: "*As Adapa, sage of Eridu, I am Ea's incarnation priest, and I am Marduk's messenger. In order to cure the patient of his illness the Great Lord Ea sent me*". What I have done is to incorporate the crucial knowledge that we have of Adapa as an exorcist into the final lines of the narrative (ending in the first person), which is exactly how those who were enacting the incantations of Adapa were to behave -, acting as 'incarnation priests', as if they themselves *were him*.

Apart from these two minor additions at the beginning and end of this translation of 'Adapa', no other extraneous elements of note need mentioning. True, I have included in this translation a Mesopotamian proverb ("*With Fate No Man Can Intervene*") to work in conjunction with the opening 'Prologue of Destiny', but then again I have also included a couple of quotes from the 'Epic of Gilgamesh' so as to frame the work - and that hardly counts as tampering with the actual text of the 'Adapa' narrative.

I am now going to do my best to demonstrate how each chapter of the story is based on the source texts, and to explain any divergences or variations.

## 0. Prologue of Destiny
### (p.3)

- In this short section, I have identified lines 1-4 of the Obverse of Tablet A as a possible 'Prologue' to the overall narrative. Because of the presence of the word 'destiny' on line one (otherwise unreadable), I made a decision to entitle this: 'Prologue of Destiny'.

- Whereas, in the Tell Haddad recension, the 'Flood Prologue' lasts around 60 lines until there is a *possible* mention of Adapa, in this Nineveh fragment the first four lines immediately introduce his most vital characteristics. He has *knowledge* and *language*, his wisdom being so great that he teaches mankind how the world functions, but (and this is his crucial deficiency) Anu has not given to him *Eternal Life*. This section, in essence, emphasizes that Adapa's destiny is to be *mortal* - for in spite of his great understanding, he is still only human. *Only Gods live forever.*

- As stated in the previous section of this essay, in this edition of *Adapa's Ascent* I have chosen *not to include* any more sizeable introductions, even though I do believe that the long prologue in the Sumerian version provides a far more substantial backdrop to the story than presented in any other recensions of 'Adapa'.

- In my opinion, the four lines at the start of A (Obverse) supply a perfect "*entrée en matière*" to the plot - even though Adapa's name is nowhere mentioned. Of course, it is possible that Adapa's name *did* figure somewhere at the start of this fragment, but given what follows and the presence of Adapa's name in the foregoing title, there is no need to name him at the outset - it is *obvious* who this passage is about.

## I. ADAPA OF ERIDU
(pp.4-6)

- In the next section, based on lines 5-14 of Fragment A, we are introduced in a more detailed way to the character and activities of Adapa. I have decided, due to *Eridu's* God being the one he serves, to identify Adapa with that town - where he acts as a practical and spiritual leader - in the title. From the beginning to the end of this chapter, Adapa is presented as one who leads his people - appearing in his priestly role.

- Though it cannot be known categorically, I take the view that Fragments A and A[1] - in that order - comprise the most likely opening passages of the Adapa narrative. We appear to have been blessed by chance, for what is missing from the beginning of the Amarna

Tablet is provided by substantially detailed (in the main well-preserved) sequences of text from A and A$^1$.

- Adapa is presented to us with an epithet with which he has become most frequently identified in a quantity of texts (not only those feeding into this story), namely: *'The Sage'*. Just as he is introduced to us in the opening 'Prologue' as wise, knowing, and skilled with words, so also do these qualities continue to be emphasized within the present segment of text.

- Looking at the Tell Haddad recension, the lines from 65-100 are all damaged to such an extent that it is impossible to make continuous sense of them. It *is possible* that some comparable description is made of him there, but it does not seem to be the case - at least on the basis of those symbols deciphered.

## II. UPON THE WIDE SEA
(pp.7-8)

- In this section, derived from lines 15-23 of Fragment A, we are introduced to another facet of Adapa - as a 'man of action'. He is presented as a fisherman (even hunter) though the focus is on his fishing ventures at sea. But more on his maritime exploits *anon*.

- This section of text also ensures that we remain aware that what Adapa does, he does for his God Ea (Enki, who is his father) and we are told of a number of tasks that he does while his divine father is resting. It is as if a father has sent out a son to do the jobs that he, as the parent, no longer desires to do - but wishes for his own blood to continue and finish.

- This section is important as it takes us to the verge of the first chief action of this epic - with which the Amarna Tablet (B) commences : Adapa's boat being capsized by Ninlil, leading to his casting of a *curse*.

- The final two lines of A are so damaged that the second to last line is only partly legible and the last line cannot be read at all. Interestingly, an additional tablet exists (Fragment A[1]) on which are to be found near-duplicates of the last 9 lines of Fragment A, yet here its final two lines are missing except for the word 'fish'. Otherwise, every word is the same and the distribution of symbols along the lines is identical. With *that* final discernible word, however, I have decided to postulate two possible closing lines.

- One feature of this section to comment on, is that when the word 'Sea' is used, what is meant is more like an expansive lagoon or the word 'See' as used in the German language - meaning 'lake'. The reality is that Eridu was a port city, but at some point between the 3rd to 2nd Millennium BCE the water dried up and Eridu ended up being isolated by land on all sides. Because the episodes on the waters are so fundamental, I think it is helpful to visualize what kind of sea is being described. If you combine the vision of a lake - so wide you cannot see the other side of it - with that of a well-vegetated lagoon, I think this

comes close to the body of water that is being described right here. If it is a lake, it is so big that you
could be floating in your boat at the centre of it yet be
unable to see any of its banks, even on the horizons.
This is why the word 'Sea' is also good in English, because it gives us the experience of expanse - "being at
sea" - which means so much, in fact, in any tongue. If
you look at maps of southern Iraq, *before* (c. 2000
BCE) and *today*, you will see Eridu *was* surrounded
by sea, whereas *now* it is landlocked. Many boats set
sail from its port in ancient times when it was continuous with the sea. Now, it is the most barren of deserts.

## III. ADAPA'S DESCENT
### (p.9)

- At this point, I have decided *not* to go straight
ahead and provide a translation of the commencing
scene of the Amarna Tablet (B), where Adapa is cursing the South Wind. To my mind, this makes too
much of a jump in the story for most readers to make
sense of it. What comes next *in chronology* seemed to
make more sense, so that is how I decided to proceed.

- This third section, therefore, is based on lines 50-
54 of the Reverse of B, a passage which is written in
the first person, where Adapa is explaining to Anu
*why* he cursed the South Wind. He excuses his actions by explaining the events leading up to them. Seeing that repetition is an oft-used, even acceptable
technique, in this genre of fiction - and that in this

instance it may be justified in that it makes the story more continuous - I have settled on the passage from lines 50-54 (B, Reverse) and transposed it into the 3rd person for this chapter. This has not entailed any major degree of alteration, except for *naming* Adapa in the passage and altering the person of some verbs.

- Not only did I feel that this additional 'chapter' was justified on the grounds of increasing the narrative logic for the reader, but I also believed that it was *possible* a comparable passage could have been present in the story sequence, in one version or other.

- For some time, I felt that this addition may be unacceptable and I debated with myself on removing it; however, in the absence of this passage I just felt that the flow of the story was too unnatural and jerky. Strangely enough, it was only once I had *completed* the current translation - in the exact sequence of seventeen chapters with prologue and epilogue that you find it now - when I became aware that Ms. Sandars (translator of the 'Epic of Gilgamesh'; 1960, Penguin) had in fact made an analogous decision almost fifty years ago when she published a prose version of 'Adapa' entitled 'Adapa the Man'. She creates a passage - early in the text - commencing: "In the middle of the sea Adapa went about catching fish", which goes on to Adapa being capsized and then continues up to the point that he casts his curse upon Ninlil. Later on in her short story-style version of 'Adapa', Ms. Sandars includes Adapa's excuse to Anu (in the first person) at the same point as that occurs in the Amarna Tablet sequence, and all of this flows very well. Just when I thought that I might have *exceeded the acceptable* in terms of playing with plot order, I discovered a translation where the same sequence was arrived at independently - which certainly reassured me.

- It could be that, just as the background to Adapa's story - the 'Flood Prologue' - may not have been necessary in later versions due to the audience's general familiarity with it, so also the scene of Adapa being capsized may have been so well-known that it was not necessary to include it in the sequence every time.

- All that *might* be so, but it does not change the fact that for a new era of readers - so unfamiliar with the base mythologies and their series of events - it could be advisable *to be easy on them* and to use the materials so as to tactfully introduce them to this story in a more comfortable fashion. If a specific device or technique is not damaging to an actual text, then I do not believe that it is bad practice to go ahead and use it. In this instance, a single passage - repeated but transposed into a different tense and introduced at an earlier point in the plot sequence - seems to improve the readability of the text for new readers. And for that reason, I feel that it is permissible, even advisable.

- As regards this section, and the third page of the previous section (p.6), the Sumerian recension from

Tell Haddad does appear to supply us with recognizably similar versions of the same narrative. From lines 101-108, Adapa is presented going out on a fishing expedition, and it is clear from this passage that he is doing so for the benefit of the people of his town, or, more properly put, for his *congregation*.

- However, surprisingly - and in line with my decision to include Adapa's being drowned by the South Wind *here* - I found that this is precisely what happens in the Tell Haddad version of the story. In Prof. Cavigneaux's translation of the text into French, directly after a passage in which Adapa has been fishing at sea (lines 101-108), there follows immediately a passage in which: "*Le vent du sud [souleva] ses bourrasques*" ('The south wind [raised] its gusts'), straight after which the text proceeds to tell us that "*Adaba, le fils d'Eridu [maudit le vent du sud]*" ('Adapa, son of Eridu, [cursed the South Wind]'). Thus, the sequence of events is laid out in a very clear order there: Adapa goes fishing; the South Wind causes chaos; Adapa curses it, making its wings break; after which Kagia - vizier - reports to Lord An(u) what Adapa has done.

- With the title chosen for this section of the translation, I wanted to emphasize how Adapa's drowning in the sea here is the very opposite of his going to Heaven later. Thus I called it 'Adapa's Descent', because Adapa has descended beneath the waves and found himself, not only in the depths of the sea, but in the home territory of his father, God of Wisdom, Enki. What is not specified - and which allows for variant readings - is whether Adapa is dead or if in fact he has survived the experience of being drowned. Prof. Izre'el, in 'Adapa and the South Wind', writes that "Adapa plunged into the sea and left the world of the living, yet he was not fully dead" — it is an interesting point, and one which still deserves further scrutiny.

It is possible that Adapa was in a *transitional state*, neither alive nor dead, but about to move on to a state of death or return to life. Like Gilgamesh - once he has journeyed through the dark mountain and is in a state of limbo between knowledge of Immortality and a return to mortal life - Adapa appears to leave the ordinary world of the living behind when he is drowned in the sea. How a reader sees the events of this chapter affects how they visualize the ongoing narrative.

## IV. THE POWER OF WORDS
### (pp.10-12)

- With this section, we turn to the beginning of Fragment B, as it is based on lines 1-7 of its Obverse side. This crucial segment of the story depicts Adapa cursing the South Wind with language of such power - hence the title of this section - that she is immediately stilled and cannot blow for seven whole days.

- This is a pivotal section in the drama, for if the drowning of Adapa (caused by Ninlil) is the incident that incites his rage, the cursing of the South Wind *by him* is an action that causes the situation to escalate further. It seems to make sense to include both the *Curse* of Adapa **and** the *Outcome* (the South Wind ceasing to blow on the land) in this same section of the text. It makes the 'cause-and-effect' relationship between these two incidents more openly obvious.

- It is probably true to say this is one of the most important scenes in the story (along with that of Adapa being offered food and water in Heaven) because in this passage Adapa goes from being a mere mortal to being a mortal who can overcome a Goddess with the power of his words. At one and the same moment he masters the powers of Magic and becomes more like a Superhuman than he was up to then. It is essentially *for this* that Adapa must be brought to account — for if a mere mortal is allowed to use dark words to paralyze the powers of a God, Divinity is in trouble! As several commentators have noted - and I believe correctly so (Michałowski, Talon, Izre'el *et al.*) - the 'Adapa' narrative appears to be very much about the magical power of language, both to harm and to heal.

## V. "BRING THAT MAN HERE!"
(pp.13-14)

- This section is based on lines 7-13 of the Obverse side of Fragment B. The drama follows directly on from what Adapa has done in the preceding scene. Ninlil is not a God whose absence can go unnoticed, so as soon as Anu realizes that the South Wind is not blowing on the land as She normally does, He wants an explanation - and asks His vizier to give Him one.

- Thankfully, Fragment B is in such good condition (Obverse and Reverse), only a few lines being partially damaged, that it is possible to proceed quite confidently regarding the reliability of the text's incidents here and with a minimal need for speculation.

- Even though the majority of key passages do have a counterpart in the Tell Haddad recension, I have made the decision to translate the phrasing and vocabulary from the Amarna Tablet here as it shows a greater level of literary maturity - also, because the poetic expression is more refined than in Sumerian.

## VI. THE PROPHECIES OF ENKI - Pt. 1
### (pp.15-18)

- This section follows on directly from Anu's having ordered Llabrat to send Adapa up to Heaven, and it is based upon lines 14-28 of Fragment B (Obverse).

- *Where* Adapa is - or rather, *what state he is in* - depends in large part upon your view of his 'drowning'. Did he survive being capsized at sea? If so, is Adapa still in the land of the living? On the other hand, if you *are* of the opinion that Adapa was well and truly "drowned" (the word used in several translations) then in what way is he continuing to exist? In that case, how can he be in the 'land of the dead'

- for we are still reading about him *as if were alive*? The *third option* - as mentioned in the commentary to Chapter IV - is that Adapa is in a *transitional state*, somewhere between the living and the dead.

There is no telling a reader how they have to view things - and what I think is important to remember is that when we are reading the drama of 'Adapa', we are entering the mythical world of Mesopotamians whose entire '*Weltanschauung*' is different from ours. Perhaps Adapa - in this scene - continues to be underwater; perhaps he remains in his father's house; perhaps he is both alive *and* dead. We are not in a world of modern science and logic. In fact, we are in a fictional world - even if it was real for the authors - and there is nothing either contradictory or impossible about Adapa being in a state, half-alive and half dead. The 'story-world' has rules all of its own.

- It is true that vocabulary could have been used which obviated this ambiguity, but I believe that by ensuring the poem does not definitively indicate whether Adapa is alive or dead, the story overall may benefit. I do not want to limit the imagination of the reader when there may be several different ways of visualizing it. It might be that when the drama of 'Adapa' was originally enacted, it was obvious to the audience that he was alive or dead *or whatever*, in line with a cultural view of the time. However, from a modern reader's standpoint, I think it is fine for the audience to be in a state of suspended disbelief regarding what *state* Adapa is in.

111

- Comparing the Fragment B (Obverse) and the Tell Haddad recensions of this passage, Enki's advice is reproduced in a similar amount of detail and it appears that the speech by Adapa's father may have been fixed early on in the evolution of this story. The complete 'Advice' (which is in this version divided between Chapters VI and VIII) runs from lines 136-150 of the Sumerian version and few key details of it vary from the Akkadian — all the way down to a paradoxical 'joke', which occurs later, as predicted.

- What needs remarking on, before proceeding, is that I decided to divide this speech between two separate chapters as I felt that it is not out of keeping with the rhythm of the story to introduce an additional element of 'intercutting'. Taking a wider view of the 'Adapa' narrative, it seems to have occurred at numerous places in the original: we move from Land to Sea to Heaven, between Adapa and Enki and Anu, always with great ease - and the effect is not different from that of watching a movie that cuts back and forth between different locations, actively progressing the plotlines in the viewer's minds. In this case, it feels acceptable at this point to cut away from Enki's speech for a moment so as to introduce Anu's messenger commanding Adapa's attendance in Heaven (Chapter VII). I do understand that the purist's view may be that I have tampered with the natural order and further disrespected the source text. However, I adhere to the same philosophy throughout - which is that I believe that any alterations in order or presentation (as long as nothing is actually eliminated or fabricated) can be positive changes if they ameliorate the modern-day reader's comprehension of the work.

- You may note, in passing, that I have called this section 'The Prophecies of Enki', as I wished to emphasize that this God - with his words of advice - clearly has *premonitive power* in regard to what will occur. The truth of his predictions proves that he is a God.

## VII. BY ROYAL COMMAND
### (p.19)

- The next section, based on lines 34-36 of Fragment B (Obverse), presents us with the messenger who has been sent - on Anu's orders (*qv.* Sec. V) - to command that Adapa attend Him in Heaven, without delay.

- I have already explained why I believe it is fitting to introduce this scene here rather than at the end of Enki's monologue: cutting away from Enki's speech - only to return to it a moment later - does, I believe, make us give *more* (rather than *less*) attention to it.

- Another reason why I believe this lightning-short scene is even better placed at this point, is because the messenger from Anu is confirming that what Enki is prophesying - up to now - *is true*. Adapa has just been notified that he is about to go and visit Anu in Heaven, and in this scene he is visited by an emissary of Anu who tells him about the command to attend.

## VIII. THE PROPHECIES OF ENKI - Pt. II
### (pp.20-21)

- This section - based on lines 28-34 of Fragment B (Obverse) - continues where Chapter VI left off. One reason why I believe this passage of text works better on its own, is because it is the central piece of advice that Enki decides to give to Adapa - regarding *what he should do when offered food and water in Heaven.* This part of Enki's speech to Adapa is quite distinct from the previous series of predictions about what the Gods - Dumuzi and Gizzida - will say to him and how he should respond to their questions, one by one. The difference is that the prophecies that Enki is making now - and his words of counsel - now relate to the most important choice with which Adapa will be faced: *whether to accept* what Anu offers to him.

- This episode of the narrative moves us onto a different stage of the story. Even if I had not interrupted Enki's prophecies with the intervening scene - wherein Anu's messenger commands Adapa to attend in Heaven - the reader would still become aware that Enki's counsel is now on a different level than that which he was giving before. Enki's previous advice was very much a prediction of what the Gods Dumuzi and Gizzida would say - even down to a specific joke - while the advice being given now is *serious.* That joke somehow marks a division-point between the two halves of Enki's monologue, and the inclusion of an intervening scene (Chapter VII) helps underline this.

- Two other observations occur to me on reading this second half of Enki's advice to Adapa: *firstly*, that Adapa is totally silent throughout, for he listens and does not question a word that he is told. — Are we to suppose that this is because he knows that he must do as Enki says, not only because this is his Father, but because He is a God? - By this point, Adapa has already infringed upon the powers of the Gods by cursing Ninlil. Does Adapa say nothing in opposition to Enki's advice because he already knows that he must do as he says, unquestioningly, in order to get back in good standing with the Gods, above all with Anu? Or is it a dramatic ploy of the authors of this drama:— not to give us a hint as to whether Adapa will obey?

*Secondly*, depending upon a reader's interpretation of previous scenes, their views of the advice offered by Enki can differ. If Adapa *has survived* Ninlil's capsizing his boat, then Adapa's not accepting the food and water from Anu would result in him not gaining Eternal Life, but he would still continue to live as a human. If, on the other hand, our understanding of Chapter III is that Adapa *has indeed perished* - or is merely in a *transitional state* between life and death - then is it not malicious in the extreme for Enki to advise Adapa against accepting gifts which would enable him to continue being alive, and without which he may fully die? — Would it be *so terrible*, for **this** God, that his son attain Eternal Life, to the extent that *he would actually prefer that his son would die instead?*

## IX. JOURNEY TO THE GREAT ABOVE
(pp.22-24)

- In the next section - based on lines 37-46 of Fragment B (Reverse) - Adapa immediately sets out on his way to Heaven. Just as the visit of the messenger in Chapter VII confirmed that Enki was correct in his prophecy about Adapa's journey to Heaven - so does this segment of text straight away reveal how right Enki has been in his precise predictions about who will meet Adapa and what they will say to him. Dumuzi and Gizzida ask him exactly the questions that were foreseen by Enki - and Adapa answers each of them exactly the way Enki advised that he should. Seeing that he does everything as he has been advised to by Enki, we as readers may be inclined to believe that Adapa will continue to follow the advice regarding gifts he will be offered. As we leave this episode, I believe that most readers could be of the view that Adapa *will do* what Enki says. I think that the element of suspense, while reading this, is not so much about what Adapa will do in Heaven — but what Anu will do once Adapa has followed the advice of Enki.

## X. IN THE PALACE OF KING ANU
(pp.25-27)

- In the following section, based on lines 46-56 of Fragment B (Reverse), Adapa finds himself in the presence of Anu, the Supreme God, and the pressure

is on for him to answer for his actions toward Ninlil.
- In the Sumerian text also, Adapa is welcomed into
Heaven, indeed, he is offered a seat to sit on by Anu.

- Having heard how Adapa will visit Heaven (predicted by Enki in Chapters V and VII), and having
witnessed the command of Anu's being conveyed by
His messenger in Chapter VI - in this scene, the moment of Adapa's reckoning has arrived. His response
to Anu's demand to know why Adapa acted as he did,
is to give his account of what Ninlil did *to him* when
he was fishing. Adapa's story of what happened to
him at sea is now provided to us in the first person,
just as it appears in lines 50-54 (B, Reverse). We
have - as explained in the commentary on Chapter III
- read an almost identical text already due to inclusion of the same scene (albeit it in the third person)
at that earlier point. As stated before, I believe that
an element of recapitulation is in keeping with the
kind of repetition that occurs in these types of work.

- Turning to the Tell Haddad recension, there are a
couple of observations to make that may be relevant,
at least in terms of how one visualizes the exchange
that is occurring in this episode. On line 173 of this
version it says that: "*An, dans l'assemblée, s'adressa
aux grands dieux*" ('Anu, in the assembly, addressed
himself to the great gods'). He then asks the question
of Adapa: Why has he broken the wings of the South
Wind? What is noteworthy here is that Anu does not
address Adapa directly but through the 'Great Gods'

- which could refer to Dumuzi and Gizzida ('Ningish-zida') but also to other Gods: Enlil, Ninhursaga *et al.* We do not witness Adapa answering An(u) directly in this version, but we read that: "*Les grands dieux répondirent à An*" ('The Great Gods responded to Anu'). Without going into their response - which includes Enki having to make up for what Adapa has done (like a parent being punished for their child's misbehavior) - what I gain from these few lines is that a Supreme God (Anu) and mortals (like Adapa) do not speak to each other directly, but only through other, mediating Gods. Reading the Sumerian version of this passage, it confirmed the way that I had come to visualize the scene in the Akkadian version.

While reading the present chapter, I think it is vital to realize that Anu is not addressing Adapa directly but through Dumuzi and Gizzida as intermediaries. Progressing through the passage, we read clearly that (my translation): "*Dumuzi and Gizzida stood beside him - to Anu his side of the story reciting*". What the general description makes me envision, is something similar to a court situation - where Anu is in the role of a Judge and the other Gods are fulfilling the roles of Counsel, who transmit their client's views to the Judge (thus indirectly). In the passage mentioned above (p.25) it is as if Dumuzi and Gizzida were presenting Adapa's version of events to Anu — much as if they were pleading for Him to show mercy to their 'client' (Adapa) and not punish him.

## XI. "WHY ?"
### (p.28)

- Even though the preceding section ends with Anu being calmed by what He has heard, Chapter XI - based upon lines 57-60 of Fragment B (Reverse) - shows us Anu in a state of considerable annoyance at how Enki has caused Adapa to behave as he did. From the wording in the passage, it is not possible to say for sure whether Anu is angry with Enki because He believes that Enki instigated Adapa's cursing the South Wind in some way, or whether He simply blames Enki for handing on some traits of character he has: *wisdom*, yet also the hot-headed atti- tude which is what has caused Adapa to "lose it" and lash out at the South Wind with a mighty curse.

- This passage is interesting because it shows how Anu does have some understanding - even *sympathy* - for the situation that Adapa finds himself in, for after Adapa's words of explanation (conveyed tactfully to Anu by Dumuzi and Gizzida) Anu appears to make a distinction between what Adapa has done - cursing the South Wind - and what the ultimate causes of this action may be. Perhaps Anu believes that Enki, acting with delicate tact, may have exerted some control over Ninlil, causing the South Wind to raise her storm-forces and ignite Adapa's rage. Who is to say how the agencies of the Gods interacted here ? In Worlds of Gods and Fiction *anything is possible*.

119

- Enki is about to have an even greater impact on the story because of the advice he has given to his son: will Adapa listen to it or will he ignore it? His doing so, or not, will determine what Anu's action are also. Thus, even if Enki is only in the background - as the one who influences Adapa through fatherly advice - he is affecting what is happening even while absent.

## XII. - GIFTS IMMORTAL -
(pp.29-31)

- Here we arrive at what is undoubtedly the most famous scene of all: where Adapa is offered the *food and water of life* by Anu. It is based on lines 60-67 of Fragment B (Reverse) and all that happens in this scene has been *foreseen* and *predicted* by Enki in Chapter VIII.

- *Apologies* - I correct myself, for what I have said above is not exactly the case. The *offer* of gifts by Anu has been predicted by Enki, but Adapa's father advises him to accept two of them while rejecting two others. Therefore *he has not predicted everything* that will occur. Enki can see (with his power of foresight) *what will happen* in Heaven, but he is clearly nervous about *how Adapa will respond* or he would not be giving his son such firm advice in Chapter VIII.
— *Or could he predict how Adapa would react too?*

- Although numerous variant translations have been tried, I have opted to use the general words 'food' and 'water', instead of more specific terms like 'bread' for the former, or 'wine' for the latter. There is even a suggestion, in Fragment E (line 2, Reverse), that a word such as 'beer' could be appropriate in place of water. To my mind, it is better to leave the words more general so that the reader has more space to visualize what they think is intended. Certainly, it is possible that something more specific is meant and that 'water' could have been a beverage like wine or beer and that 'bread' could be a suitable choice of sustenance to substitute for the generic word 'food'.

- When the gifts were spoken of in Chapter VIII by Enki, I decided to call them the "food of death" and "water of death". I did not use the words 'deadly', 'lethal' or 'fatal' as adjectives to describe the food and water, although these were viable alternate choices. I decided to use the phrases above because I wanted to contrast - in the clearest way possible - what Enki has foretold will be offered to Adapa, and what is actually offered to him: namely, the "food of life" and the "water of life". I felt that in this way, the difference between what is predicted - and what is actually offered - is as plain as it can be. Adapa is warned about one thing, yet in fact he is offered another — that is obvious. What this section goes on to show us, however, is that Adapa is not prepared to ignore his father, for he rejects the food and water as advised.

- To begin discussing the alternative viewpoints on this passage (and Enki's advice) is sadly out of the question here as it would be like opening a veritable "can of worms" — indeed, debating the meaning of this passage alone seems to have become a sub-genre of 'Adapa' scholarship in itself. One of the key questions being asked is: *Why did Enki deceive Adapa - telling him to refuse what could give him Eternal Life?* — Some have asserted that it was indeed deceitful, and that this is part of Enki's wily nature. Others have argued that Enki only advises Adapa against partaking of the gifts of food and water because - being the food and water of the Gods - they would be poisonous to a human being; indeed, *would be the death of him.* Although there is no space for debate here, when I read this section and reflect on how Enki's advice has influenced Adapa, I wonder whether Enki - as father - simply did not want his son to attain the same status (being a God) as him: *the Father who is not prepared to accept his Son as a fully mature Man.* On the other hand, I also wondered whether Enki gave his advice as a bit of a game between him and Anu - a battle of loyalties - to see whether Adapa will do as his father says or be persuaded by Anu to accept His gifts. A whole book could be written about this scene in Heaven alone. It is so redolent with meanings and mythical significance of many kinds — which is why I believe it is such a dangerous topic to even begin discussing!

- Looking at the equivalent passage in the Tell Haddad recension, there are several variations to note. Firstly, the episode opens with a line that is lacking in the Amarna Tablet (though I have not chosen to include it in this translation). On line 166 - after Dumuzi and Gizzida introduce Adapa to Anu, it states: "*An donna à Adaba, le sage, l'intelligent, un siège en signe de bienvenue*" ('Anu gave Adapa the wise, the intelligent, a place to sit as a sign of welcome'). What I notice in this version, is that Adapa not only refuses the bread and water, but also the clothes he is offered - yet he *does accept* the oil. This is significant as it means that the acceptance of two gifts and the rejection of two others - as in the Amarna Tablet - had not been fixed in the narrative by that time. However, reading lines 138-142 (Tell Haddad), what Adapa does here conforms with the advice that he has been given by Enki. In that version, Adapa has been warned not to accept the clothes he is offered and *only* to accept the oil from the four gifts offered.

- What stands out most to me, in this chapter, is the way that Anu responds to Adapa's refusal of gifts - *by laughing*. Although He has been rebuffed, Anu does not behave as if He has been gravely insulted but "*He just laughs and He asks*" Adapa a question about why he refused. At this point, it does not appear to have crossed Anu's mind that someone else had advised Adapa not to accept the gifts that he is offered. In subsequent scenes, however - Chapters XIV and XV, based on the 'Nineveh Fragments' - Anu seems to realize what Enki has done, in terms of convincing Adapa with advice. There, He is angry and upset about how He and Adapa have been treated by Enki.

## XIII. BANISHED FROM THE HEAVENS
(pp.32-33)

- Within this chapter, the final lines of cuneiform are translated from the Amarna Tablet. This episode, which is the concluding one in that version, is based upon lines 67-71 of Fragment B (Reverse). Anu, even after hearing from Adapa that he *only* refused the food and water of life *because of the advice* given to him by Enki, orders that Adapa be sent back to Earth for rejecting what he has been offered: "*Send him hence back to his world for he does not belong here with Gods Immortal*". As this scene is present at the closure of the most complete and undamaged version of the 'Adapa' narrative (Amarna), it has been treated as if it were *the* universally accepted conclusion to the story. But the truth is that we have been presented with numerous versions of the story - each written at a different period of time - and none can claim absolute precedence over the others. But as far as encyclopaedias and guides on literature are concerned, Adapa's ejection from Heaven is *the story's* **usual ending**, even though other conclusions have been known for decades, some only emerging recently.

- As far as the Amarna recension is concerned, this passage - as an ending to the drama - does make a lot of sense. The few lines of prologue (Obverse of tablet) emphasized that Adapa had been given *Wisdom*, but not *Eternal Life*, and with this ending, Adapa's being ejected from Heaven *is due to his being Human* - and by virtue of that, unable to possess Eternal Life. The dichotomy of Gods and Mortals is straightforward in the Mesopotamian era: Gods are Immortal, Humans are Mortal; Gods live forever, Humans live only their transient lives. Sure, a human can be wise, and Adapa can be extra-wise - yet that does not qualify him for being Immortal; even being the son of a God does not mean he can be Immortal himself. All this is underscored by the ending to Fragment B, which is what is presented in this, the 13th chapter.

- Arriving at this point in the story, I think that the audience (*then* and *now*) may in fact harbour sympathy for Adapa because of the way he has been led to reject Eternal Life by his father Enki. Yet at the same time, I think that many will recognize that Adapa is not a mere puppet of any God, for when he wanted to bring down a God - all on his own - Adapa had no problem in paralysing the powers of Ninlil.

- Looking at the ending of the earliest (Tell Haddad) recension, and that of the Amarna tablet, they really are very different affairs. While in the latter, Adapa is banished from Heaven by Anu, in the former version there is no mention of this at all. Instead (on l.172) An(u) complains how Enki has prevented Him from being able to give Life to Adapa and the story ends, not with Adapa being ejected from Heaven, but with Enki being ordered to make good Ninlil's wings, followed by an incantation to 'Ea' as a Divine Healer.

- It only remains for me to remark that the final line of the Amarna Tablet - on which source the present chapter is almost entirely based (Reverse) - is in fact missing, and I have had to hypothesize what those words might have been. After line 70 - which I have translated as, "TAKE HIM AWAY FROM ME ! SEND HIM HENCE BACK TO HIS WORLD!" - there is one line that appears to be absent. With poetic licence, perhaps, yet based upon the spirit of the Prologue to Fragment A (Obverse), I decided to end this section with the words: "FOR HE DOES NOT BELONG HERE WITH GODS IMMORTAL". These words seemed appropriate because they state explicitly the implicit reason that Adapa is now being evicted from Heaven.

## XIV. - DEAR ENKI -
(pp.34-36)

- This chapter is the main one in which I have decided to venture upon the translation of verses which, although there *is* some positive basis for them in the source materials, nonetheless the end result has required a significant degree of conjecture in order to produce it. In this segment of *Adapa's Ascent*, I come far closer to the wilder flights of speculation on which I have launched in the 'Translation Sketch of a Sumerian Text' (*qv.* Appendix 4), although I do not regret doing so, as I think this section may come close to re-p- resenting the substance of a portion of text which has not yet been discovered in an undamaged version.

- This additional episode of 'Adapa' is based on the entirety of Fragment C (lines 1-19), the main disadvantage of this source being that the beginning of most of the lines are damaged, and working out what is written on them requires a great deal of guesswork. However, I think that Prof. Shlomo Izre'el makes a plausible proposition when he states in his study 'Adapa and the South Wind'(p.36) that: *"Perhaps Ea was summoned by a messenger to Anu to discuss the situation after Anu was told of Adapa's mischief"*. What occurs in this scene is in keeping with the text on which the following chapter is based, for lines 4-6 of Fragment D (Reverse) speak frankly of Anu's outrage that another God should consider himself permitted to behave in such a disruptive way — and it is clear from the context that Enki is the one referred to.

- Only after composing Chapter XIV - much in the form that you find it now - did I discover the above remarks of Prof. Izre'el, and I can only say that I was relieved to see that I may not be the only one who considers this kind of scene could once have existed. I am encouraged by the openness that exists within the community of 'Adapa' scholarship, that there are expectations to discover - due to any of a number of excavations being successful - new sources supporting theories about that work, or that add new material to the narrative as we know it. In fact, I think there is an awareness that we may be surprised, any day, by a version of 'Adapa' quite different from any we possess.

- I have done my best to ensure that the language of
this chapter is in keeping with the following chapter,
as well as with the words pronounced by Anu within Chapter XI - based on lines 57-60 of Fragment B
(Reverse) - where He expresses anger and annoyance
that someone has caused Adapa to behave as he has.
I believe that I have managed to recreate the same
tenor of language in these three chapters, though
there was a greater mass of material to play with in
composing this chapter as Fragment C is substantial.

- The difference that I think some readers will notice,
is that whereas speeches in Chapters XI and XV are
very much rhetorical in nature, the tone of this chapter is quite different. While in those two chapters,
Anu's displeasure was very clearly pointed toward
Enki - albeit in his absence - in this chapter the communication with Enki is *more direct*. Anu's words -
although conveyed to Enki by a herald - are addressed
straight to Enki, though in a respectful, diplomatic
way. *How* and *Why* Enki has led his son Adapa to
behave in such a way when he visited Heaven, is seriously queried by Anu here. Why was Adapa given
*such strict demands* in terms of the advice he was
given prior to visiting Anu? This passage attempts to
flesh out Anu's bewilderment at what Enki has done.

- What really stands out to me, in terms of the material on which Chapters XI, XIV and XIV have been
based, is the large degree to which Anu's initial fury

with Adapa - for neutralizing the power of the South Wind - has so greatly softened that He is even regretful of throwing him from Heaven and appears to be on the verge of reversing His decision at this stage.

- What also especially strikes me about these same three chapters of material - taken as a whole - is the great amount of respect that seems to be afforded to Adapa by Anu. For even though it is true that he was *commanded* to appear before Him, there is considerable disbelief - from Anu's side - either that Adapa would have cursed the South Wind if there were no other influencing factors, or that Adapa would have refused the gifts that he has been offered if he had not been advised against doing so by someone else. Adapa is given the "benefit of the doubt", both in terms of his actions and intentions, though he does appear to be more deserving of sympathy for the way that Enki may have deceived him than for losing his temper with Ninlil. I think that he is *more responsible* for cursing the South Wind than for refusing the gifts of Anu. In the former case, he made a rash decision in his fury - it seems fair for *him* to be held to account. It was not Enki who cast a curse.

- It will be noted that I have not gone along with all the words exatly as presented in this source — at least on those lines legible enough to be deciphered, that is. For example, in several places - in order to arrive at something that is more intelligible - I have chosen to ignore the *person* and *tenses* of the verbs as they appear. I am aware of the syntactical deficiencies of this section in particular, but it was more important to me that this chapter represented *the spirit* of the segment of text which it translated than that it be pedantically correct in terms of its grammatical accuracy.

- Looking at all the possible places that the material from Fragment D would be most appropriate, this is where I felt it was best suited in terms of the plot. Perhaps it could also have worked after Chapter XV, but I think that it fits more discreetly *beforehand* - prior to Anu's greater outpouring of anger at the God who has been so arrogant to suppose that he is more powerful than Him. With the emergence of further material in future - perhaps even other versions of the episode on which this chapter has been based - it is possible that another position for it might be found.

## XV. "WHO AMONG GODS?"
### (p.37)

- After this lucid communication with Enki - via Anu's envoy - the following chapter shows us Anu's greater level of fury at what has happened. In the passage that is translated from lines 4-6 of Fragment D (Reverse), Anu's annoyance boils over into rage. He is fuming that another God has thought himself more powerful — it reveals a side of the story which is *the contention of powers between the Gods.* Anu is aware that Enki has outwitted Adapa and Him *with words.*

- This was a more straightforward passage to translate than the previous one, as D is in good condition - only the beginning of several lines being damaged beyond recognition (as well as the last two lines). The three lines from which this chapter have been taken, however, are totally legible and it has been possible - without indulging in heavy speculation - to arrive at a clear sense of their meaning and to set them in poetry.

- So much has been said about Chapters XI, XIV and XV already - due to having discussed them as a group in the previous sub-section of this commentary - that there is no need to say anything more here. I believe that this passage is very important as it shows Anu's awareness of the competition that Enki is waging with Him, in terms of controlling the decisions of a mortal - in this case Adapa. I do think that C and D benefit from being looked at closely together, as they appear to overlap in their interpretation of the story and for this reason - at least in my opinion - it feels as if they were from the *selfsame version* of the 'Adapa' story.

## XVI. ADAPA'S ASCENT
### (pp.38-39)

- The current chapter - based on lines 7-11 of Fragment D (Reverse) - is very much the climactic episode of the 'Adapa' narrative. It relates how Anu restores Adapa to Heaven and gives him a permanent place there among the Gods - a *complete reversal* of how the Amarna Tablet ended, which was presented in Chapter XIII.

- If we turn to the first versions of the Adapa narrative (Tell Haddad), we will be reminded that at this early stage in the evolution of a myth, Adapa was not banished from Heaven for refusing the gifts of Anu. Enki is given orders to repair the wings of the South Wind and to see to it that Ninlil be restored in her place - but there is neither punishment of Adapa for having cursed her, nor denial of Eternal Life for refusing the gifts offered to him. In fact, the only phrase spoken by Anu regarding 'life', is that "*Enki* [...] *has stopped me from giving him* [Adapa] *my life*" ('Enki [...] m'a empeché de lui donner ma vie'). Though it *may be implied* - because Anu is a God - that 'my life' means 'my eternal life', but even this much is not expressed so definitely in the Sumerian recensions of the drama. Banishment from Heaven is not part of this version, and after the above statement by Anu (line 171) there is no further mention of Adapa in the remaining seventeen lines of the final tablet.

- Turning to the text of *this* chapter, it has similarities with a scene of transfiguration in the New Testament - thinking of the passage about Jesus during Matthew 17. Here, Adapa is raised up to Heaven by Anu and it is made clear that he will occupy a place among the Gods henceforth. This is a very bold and exciting end to the drama and it seems to be like a demonstration *by Anu* that He is the one who "wears the shoes" in Heaven - that He will not have Adapa's Destiny be determined by Enki's sly interference.

- It appears to me to be like a third stage in the evolution of the Adapa narrative - though there may be more, of course. While the Tell Haddad version (discussed on the preceding page) shows us Anu giving Enki orders to repair the South Wind (making no further mention of Adapa), the Amarna recension has developed the story to a new and very different level: Adapa being banished from Heaven for refusing the gifts of Eternal Life. However, by the time of the 7th Century BCE, the Nineveh Fragments appear to reveal a further transformation of the story in the form of the episode presented in this chapter - Adapa being 're-welcomed' into Heaven and becoming, like the Gods, resident there. All that is not stated, is whether - by assuming Immortality - Adapa has become a God himself. His name has not yet been discovered on any Mesopotamian list of figures who have been deified. It is possible that he was considered to be one who occupies a special place halfway between Gods and Man, as the special figure of the 'First Exorcist'.

- There is no room here to write about the religious growth that takes place within Sumeria and Babylonia over the period of one millennium, nor to speculate on how those changes impacted the narratives of the 'Adapa' drama - for there is too much material to cover and too many directions in which investigation could lead. All I can remark, purely on the basis of the source materials for the current translation, is that some kind of development in the personalities and potencies of the Gods - and also in the character of Adapa - appears to take place between the varying versions. Anu, though always a God of deep understanding, seems more forthright and powerful by the time we reach the Nineveh texts. Enki becomes even more skilled in his powers of prophecy and wisdom, while Adapa goes from playing second fiddle to Enki (in the Sumerian texts) to being the truly central and focal character of the drama - to the extent that there is no question but to name the entire story after him.

- Turning, lastly, to the title of this drama again, it needs mentioning now as it has also been used as the title to this particular chapter. 'Adapa's Ascent' seemed to me the most appropriate title to give to this passage of text as this is specifically what we are seeing represented during this episode — *Adapa's Ascent into Heaven*. It is the 180° opposite to the scene that was presented in Chapter IV of this translation ('Adapa's Descent') - for whereas *there* he was drowned in the watery depths of Lord Enki, *here* he is raised up to the celestial heights of the Supreme God, Anu. Most of *Adapa's Ascent*, in fact, talks about 'Heaven' or takes place there. Either Anu is calling for Adapa from Heaven (IV), Enki is predicting what will happen there (VI and VIII), Adapa is on his way up (IX) or he is actually there with Lord Anu (X-XIII). However, it is not until this chapter that he is fully welcomed into Heaven and made one of its pantheon. — 'Adapa's Ascent' is the apotheosis of this narrative.

# XVII. 'SO BE IT'
## (p.40)

- The final chapter proper - Chapter XVII - is based on lines 12-14 of Fragment D (Reverse) and is nothing more than the plot of the 'Adapa' story *in nuce*. With three lines of text, the Nineveh author summarizes the drama of the myth: *firstly*, it is emphasized that Adapa was a human; *secondly*, we are reminded that Adapa "broke the wing of the South Wind"; and *thirdly*, it is recapitulated that, at the culmination of this tale, Adapa is raised up to Heaven like a God.

- These seem to be the ideal lines with which to close the work, mirroring the 'pseudo-text' with which I introduced the myth on pages 0-1 - lines which, although they were based on materials about Adapa, were not from any of the key sources of the tale. That this Nineveh Fragment (D) closes with such a clear round-up of the plot, seems to re-emphasize what the core of the plot was *by that time* (7th Century BCE): that of a mortal, so mighty as to be able to overpower a God, ultimately ascending to join their company.

- Line 14 closes with the three short words "so be it", much like placing the words 'Amen' at a prayer's end. These words indicate the religious value of the text. Whether wholly or in part, 'Adapa' has elements of being an 'origins tale' about the healing abilities of the *Exorcist*, a revered priest with curing power who is like *Adapa reincarnated* while doing an exorcism.

## <u>00. Epilogue - The Invocation</u>
### (pp.41-42)

- With this section, based on lines 15-23 of Fragment D (Reverse), we finally find ourselves at the very end of the 'Adapa' drama as a whole. As remarked before, the earliest known recension of this narrative (Tell Haddad; 18th Century BCE) and the most recent version of 'Adapa' (Nineveh; 7th Century BCE) both close with such an incantation. The interesting difference is that whereas in the former case the story concludes with a prayer to Enki, in the latter case the drama culminates instead with an invocation to Adapa. This seems to indicate an elevation in the status of Adapa, such that even if he has not been raised to the level of a God, nonetheless he is being revered as one who is capable of: relieving the ills of the world, removing sickness and healing the afflicted of all kinds.

- What has been remarked on, particularly in more recent years, is how important a figure Adapa was as the prototype of the Exorcist (Cavigneaux; Milstein; Annus *et alia*). It has emerged, from various sources - including prayers, guides for exorcism, holy rites - that Adapa was one whose very name could be used to vanquish evil, much in the same way that Christians use "The Name of Christ" so as to chase demons from the body of one who is believed to be possessed. Indeed, it has been revealed that Exorcism Priests were actually considered to be 'Incarnation Priests' - ones who actually *became* Adapa whilst performing their rites.

- The poor condition of this cuneiform fragment is, of course, a particular challenge in the interpretation of this text. It is impossible to make out the beginnings of most of the lines and the final two lines are thoroughly illegible. I have referred to all of the attempts to decipher this segment of 'Adapa' and I have found the versions of Profs. Philippe Talon and Shlomo Izre'el especially helpful. At the same time, I have gained a wider view of this passage by referring back to the Sumerian edition of the narrative (lines 182-190) - even though its closing incantation is addressed to Enki and not to Adapa. I am aware of how my verse becomes highly speculative here, and I am acutely conscious - in trying to make the text read *as if complete* - that I may have sent my arrows far from the target, if not in the wrong directions.

- I have just a few words to say regarding my understanding of the sickness, spoken of in this passage. It is my belief that when the text is speaking of illness and evils, these two broad terms are to include: (a) physical illness; (b) mental illness (seen by them as a 'possession' by evil spirits); and (c) wide-ranging, mass-ravaging epidemics. As far as *this* text is concerned, I think it is specially speaking about the last -mentioned type of sickness - in the form of *plagues.* Dr. Tholozan, in his article 'Une épidémie de la peste en Mésopotamie 1867', points at the existence of such illness in the period preceding the first versions of 'Adapa' - when there was even a 'God of the Plague', in the form of *Nergal*. Plagues are, for sure, familiar from several books of the bible such as Deuteronomy, Exodus and Samuel, so I do not believe that it is an outlandish misinterpretation. It makes sense to me that - not just so as to cure an individual who is suffering, but to stop a 'Pest' from decimating a great many people - *Adapa's Name* should be invoked in order to repel or destroy the 'Evil'. I believe that it is quite plausible that the kind of disease being spoken of in this passage is some kind of plague, and whether or not it was an airborne epidemic, it does seem credible that Mesopotamians may have truly believed that illness was sent by the Wind, perhaps even the South Wind - yet with Adapa's intervention it could be stopped from blowing malevolently on the people.

- As explained on p.99, I have taken the liberty of including an explicit exhortation of 'Adapa' at the end of this chapter, in a way that I believe is in keeping with the source - in place of the missing lines 22-23.

- Once the main text of Adapa has established that he ultimately gained Immortality, this invocation does something different - it points to his *acquisition of divine transcendence* as being at the basis of the exorcists' powers - and they can only heal when they are possessed by that *spirit of Adapa*. "An ill wind blows no good", yet Adapa is master of Ninlil, welcomed into the circle of Gods by Anu: *his very name is sacred* and need only be invoked for someone to be cured.

## MINOR POINTS AND ADDITIONAL SOURCES

- And that is where my poetic translation of 'Adapa' reaches its conclusion. In spite of the existence of other texts - such as Fragment E, lines 1-3 of Fragment D, and further fragments that have been published (*qv.* Jeremiah Peterson *et al.*) - I cannot discover anything additional in the sources that I believe would augment the content of any sections in a substantial way.

- Although none of its text is translated in *this poem*, the Tell Haddad versions have been invaluable in helping to make decisions on numerous issues in this translation. As mentioned before, I decided to keep my 'Translation Sketch of a Sumerian Text' separate from the main poetic work as the former is dangerously speculative and I have taken a different approach there, in the way that I have composed the passages. I think that other readers will also find that a reading of those texts does add to one's perspective of the 'Adapa' legend, especially in terms of the extra incidents and the different level of focus on Adapa.

- A last remark to make is that, when it came to the use of names in *Adapa's Ascent*, I have opted to use the Akkadian forms wherever possible, although I have - on several occasions - used the Sumerian form of Enki ('Ea') when this fitted better with the sound of words. I would have done the same with 'Anu' if needed (using 'An' where preferable) but I have only used His name in that way in the 'Sumerian Sketch'.

# Concluding _Adapa's Ascent_

IT SEEMED TO ME AS IF the process of _composition_ (and afterwards _re-evaluation_) of what I had written, would never end. Every new book and research paper touching on 'Adapa' revealed fresh perspectives on this archetypal myth - so I kept delaying the completion of the book as I felt hesitant about finalizing it. New data and findings kept altering my views of the source texts - especially of their purpose.

However, even though I am still as ardently interested in what will be investigated and analyzed next by the Assyriologists, I shall **never** possess any of the depth in learning and years of experience that they do in their understanding of cuneiform writing. I am nothing but apologetic that - being so slight of an academic - I have produced a work that is so very flawed. It is filled with faults and failings that will be instantly visible to those who are scholarly experts - yet in spite of that I was compelled to produce it.

I have almost arrived at the moment in time that I am ready - yet with the sadness of parting from a friend - to leave _Adapa's Ascent_ behind. **Adapa** has been like a companion to me, but I have reached the point that I can accompany him no more. Allow me, therefore, at this crossroads - where I am about to part from this work - to make my closing remarks on this translational task. My analytical explications of the text are over. All I want to speak of now is my own attitude to this work: what I tried to achieve.

I knew, from the moment I embarked on it, that I had set myself too ambitious a task. However, once the idea took grip of me - to attempt to synthesize a *'Gesamtwerk'* from the numerous versions of 'Adapa' existing - I could not shake it off, no matter what other projects I was pursuing in the mean time. However many years I left to pass, this text would not leave me alone, therefore - in the middle of this life - I decided that this job of versification needed to be completed, just so that I could go along my own path, in peace. I suspect that, if I had not concluded it now, I might be harangued by this project's insistence on getting done, even fifty years or more hence.

I know that my gung-ho attitude toward this writing task may have some of the critics frowning, but I need to emphasize that - even though this book has been published for a general audience - it was for myself that I first of all needed to produce this work. I am both the creator of *Adapa's Ascent* (as a poetic work) and at the same time my own 'audience of one' - trying to evaluate (in scholastic isolation) the point where poetry becomes one with the story and how I feel about what I have written when I read it myself.

The truth is that, ever since I discovered it, I found the 'Adapa' narrative extremely hard to understand. At the same time as it magnetized me with its pure drama of 'Man and Immortality' — it also confounded me with its ambiguities and contradictions, mysterious gaps and weighty unanswered questions. What I wanted to do was to spend more time with this impenetrable story until it did make more sense - and by setting myself the goal of creating an English translation of 'Adapa', I had an opportunity to look more deeply into the story - while not feeling guilty that I was solely indulging my own private pleasure.

*Adapa's Ascent* is - at one and the same time - both a work of translation and an original composition. Being a translator, a human being who is part of this process, it is not possible to fully absent one's own personality from the proceedings. At the end of the day, I am not a computer-system providing formulaically calculated word-equivalents of the cuneiform into English. Rather, I am a *person* who has discovered these texts, one who has multiple strands of real fascination with them, and, as I have confessed several times during this essay, I was possessed by a spirit of determination to create a unified text from the incomplete sources that span more than a millennium. In doing so, I have tried to let actual texts lead the way and not to allow my own thoughts to commandeer the material. The task of translation is less of a science than an art, and it is a process that becomes contaminated by personality because I, as a *real person*, am the one composing the story's events and ideas in a different language. How can I do so without allowing human feelings and the personal elements of my style to impact upon what I write?

All I hope is that - in spite of the unavoidably subjective nature of this task - I may somehow have been in tune with the viewpoints of its original authors. 'Adapa', in all the versions that have been found - as well as through many additional references to him in literature, correspondence and religious instructions, from the Sumerian to the Babylonian periods - appears as an archetypal and fundamental character in the mythology of the Mesopotamians. Whether his was the name of a real individual or the fusion of *several* real-life figures merged into one character (under a single name) it is impossible to say at this time. We will never see documentary footage of someone called *Adapa* — see him emerging as the leader of people after a Great Flood, see him as the Priest of Eridu, or any of the incidents in the text. All we can base our views of the past upon is the evidence we unbury and uncover in different places. The "Real Adapa" will always remain beyond grasp.

Looking at these 'Adapa' tablets as a whole - the primary sources of this translation - I think of them as being the only remaining records of a religious drama that may have been enacted in a *theater* of the Temple at Eridu. I imagine what are left as being no more than *scripts* of what was performed.

Of course, I cannot support this hypothesis with any concrete evidence, but I deem it *not implausible* that the tablets provide us with the accompanying text to a series of tableaux that were presented and acted out — with costumes, music and other appurtenances. *Man is a Dramatic Animal*, and the text, when I return to consider and reconsider it, seems more like a drama that has been recorded than like a mere *tale*. When I think to myself that 'Adapa', as a substantial and complete story, was being set down in writing as early as the 18th Century BCE, and that it was still going strong in 7th Century Akkadian - I wonder how far this myth's history stretched back into the 3rd Millennium BCE and I am simply stunned at how the story has survived into the 3rd Millennium CE!

When exactly 'Adapa' was lost from view by the civilized world, it is not entirely possible to say, but it is possible that this myth had been circulated for about three thousand years in much similar form - from the days following a Great Flood (as early as the 3rd Millennium BCE) all the way up to Roman Mesopotamia (as late as the 7th Century CE). Even though, up to now, attempts to *identify* Adam with Adapa may have been inconclusive, what *is* for sure is that 'Adapa' is an equally important representative of the myth of a "First Man" - but in a different way. While Adam (with Eve) is evicted from a 'Paradise' in which he was first created, Adapa is temporarily admitted to Heaven but loses his place there due to following bad advice, though it is open to interpretation. It is partly because they are such iconic stories of 'Origins', and about the eternal opposition between Gods and Mortals - as much as between Foolishness and Knowledge - that the 'Adam' and 'Adapa' narratives transitioned into lasting works of literature, so long ago. The only difference is that 'Adapa' has been concealed from human view for thousands of years.

Concerning this essay's subtitle - 'Recreating an Ancient Classic' - I wish to say a few words in the light of the preceding paragraphs. If we take the up-to-date Merriam-Webster Dictionary definition of a 'classic' as "a work of enduring excellence", then this does seem to be true of the 'Adapa' narrative just as much as of 'Adam and Eve'. Living in a day and age when reviewers will acclaim films such as 'The God-father' or 'Citizen Kane' as "classics" within years of being released - we are even used to being told that something *has attained this status the moment that it appears*, much as happened with 'Schindler's List'. I make this movie observation because we do not yet know whether the above works will retain their status as classics for decades or centuries - never mind beyond a millennium. Turning again to 'Adapa', however, it is clear that - in its various forms - it endured (even according to the *most conservative* estimates, based on dating the texts that we possess) before disappearing from sight for over two and a half thousand years. It is a work that has been passed down and remain relevant a long time. If longevity is one factor in a work being a *classic* , then 'Adapa' has passed the test several times moreso than 'Macbeth'. In the 1990's, Quentin Tarantino films were instantly acclaimed as classics before even a year had passed since their release - does this mean that they were **not** classics, according to *duration* being **the** defining characteristic of belonging to the pantheon of fame? — or, if they *are* classics, is it possible there are other criteria of *Immortality* regarding works of art?

I say 'Immortality' because that, in a way, is all that is meant by a work being a *classic* one - that with the passing of years *endures* and *endures*, one that with time does not fade but remains ever vivid and ***lives on***. This is what I believe is intended by the word "enduring", as used within Webster's definition of what a classic is - a work that lasts far longer than the era during which it became famous. If, on the other hand, I suppose that 'Se7en' **is** a *classic* work - in spite of its youth, owing to different criteria than mere longevity - then my focus would rather be on the second key word in that *same* dictionary definition : 'value'. This is a key factor in why we continue to read, look at or listen to something. I continue reading 'Of Mice and Men' because I *value* what I am learning from the author; I admire Michelangelo's 'David' because I recognize it's artistic *value*; and I spend time listening to something - Beethoven's 5th Symphony or an audio-recording of 'Othello' - because I derive genuine *value* during the time that I am listening to them.

If every book that was old became a classic, that would be a very strange and awkward situation indeed - for there would be so many works to choose from that it would not be possible to get to the end of reading them! It is even likely that one would not be able to begin making decisions as to which are of greater value than others. It *is* this question of 'value' that lies at the heart of why one work receives more attention over time than another. In 'Adapa' I believe that we find something that has this kind of *value*.

*What* is at the basis of a work being of value, is a larger question, for it could possess many different types of *value*, including: literary value, historical value, artistic value, scientific value, cultural value, *inter alia*. Regarding the cuneiform tablets of 'Adapa', I believe that all of the above value-types are satisfied - which are added to by its antiquity. Some works, it is true, are *only* remembered due to their age - and but for that would probably never be mentioned - yet real works of value, those we like to call "the classics", do not *need* to be old (that is only an *added factor*). It is for this reason that sometimes - often with supreme confidence - critics and reviewers are ready to acclaim a brand new work as *classic* before even a decade has passed, simply because they have experienced the artistic value it possesses and are thoroughly convinced it will be recognized for ever.

With *Adapa's Ascent*, I am making no claims whatsoever to *creating* a 'classic work' - all that I hope I have done is to open a new window onto a text from long ago, attempting to shine a fresh light onto it by casting it in English poetry. The *formidable contents* of the 'Adapa' tablets are what make it such compelling reading, not any specific forms of verse that I have set it in. It is the 'Myth of Man and Immortality', at its heart - so primal and pure in its simplicity - that make it such an everlasting work, not any elements added at the stage of translation. All one can hope for - as the translator - is to do minimal damage to the meaning of the original, yet that is hard to avoid.

I cannot make a secret of the fact that I find closure of this work of poetic translation harder than arriving at the completion of any other composition. Perhaps, in part, it is because I realize that there is *another author* (in fact, *authors*) of the original texts, and that however much accuracy and artistry I may be able to achieve in my translation of their work - into my own language - it is well-nigh inevitable that I will never be able to replicate the effects that the words had in the period when they were originated.

I can *do my best* to seek the 'maximum sense' out of each one of the extant sources - and to express it in the most natural language I am able to find - but this does not mean that I will be able to penetrate what was the spirit and purpose of the original work; I can simply *try to*, even if never-successful. I am ever aware that the gaps and flaws in my understanding of the Mesopotamians have done certain injury to the intended sense of some scenes - but I am unable to know what only a film-camera could reveal to us of what 'Adapa' *really was back then*. Without being able to return in time, there are too many things that we will never know of that culture's everyday life. What my mind visualizes of the 'Adapa' narrative may be so far from what the people were involved in - as a religious rite, performance or whatever - that there really is **no way** to equate my subjective work *with anything that ever actually existed* - yet still, *the desire to attempt to replicate something* will not go away. Thus in spite of my reservations, I continued.

My hope is that this essay will have helped readers appreciate my own point-of-view, as *author*, on what I have translated. No matter what the judgment of time is upon this particular version of the 'Adapa' legend, I hope that I have made clear how this book came together, as well as some of the choices that I made along the way, while writing it. That I have been distracted from this task repeatedly over many years *is a reality*, but now it is done - including all introductions and commentary - I would like to emphasize that I have only had **three key aims in mind**. These were: *first*, to make 'Adapa' a living text that can appeal to readers now; *second*, not to limit it to one viewpoint alone; and *third*, to translate the work *as a whole*, not focussing solely upon words and sentences but upon larger units of narrative meaning. Though I have mentioned some of these earlier, in closing I would just like to make a few final remarks on how fundamental these aims have been throughout.

*Firstly*, as far as my desire to create a new and living work out of one from the distant past, *fidelity* to the original materials has constantly been the preeminent value I have tried my hardest to adhere to. It was crucial for me that what I *re-created* would be from those *primal sources*. The challenge has been to enable those texts to speak directly to the reader of today - not appearing like ancient artifacts, so strange to the touch and impossible to discern, but more like fruit still fresh, ever vibrant with the electricity of the Mesopotamians' primal creative energies.

While it is by all means possible that versions of 'Adapa' exist which, like the 'Epic of Gilgamesh', date back to the 3rd Millennium BCE, what we do know for sure is that **we** are readers of tablets - though not of clay - living in the 3rd Millennium CE ! If the texts of 'Adapa' were not cast in words that are intelligible to a general reader today, then it is possible that audiences for this incredible story would be lost.

In creating this translation of *Adapa's Ascent*, I have been mindful that the language needs to read equally well for several groups of reader. *On the one hand,* there are scholars of Assyriology - those who have various levels of knowledge on how the Sumerians, Akkadians, Assyrians and Babylonians lived. Some of them will have extensive knowledge of these several cultures, while others may only have detailed understanding of one or other of those civilizations. *Secondly,* there are readers who, while being scholars in Assyriology, are also specialists in reading one or more of the cuneiform scripts. These readers - as well as those who have knowledge of the rituals and religions of Mesopotamia - will have a much more profound comprehension of 'Adapa' than scholars with a wide-ranging general knowledge. The *third* group of readers who need mentioning, are members of the general public who have a smattering of knowledge about ancient civilizations (from school, television, online *etc.*) and approach this text with some appreciation - limited though it may be - about the Ancient World, including Egypt, perhaps even Mesopotamia.

Finally, there is the *fourth* and largest group of readers, those who have no knowledge at all of earliest civilization - perhaps because they did not learn about it at school, or because they are young and have not yet done so. In truth, it is a failing of modern school systems, that they do not teach enough - in general - about the ancient world, and when they do so, it is almost entirely restricted to the Greeks and Romans.

I mention these groups, only as examples, for of course there are really many other types of readers to include here. - The real challenge of writing a text that can be read by such diverse audiences of readers, is that the vocabulary used (and the styles exercised) need to speak equally to them all. Though I have done my best to strike a balance that may be acceptable to these groups - keeping scholars, learners and general public (including children) alike, in mind - it is impossible to know whether I have succeeded in any way. All I can say is that if I hear, some time hence, that various groups of reader are complaining that the language of this translation is inappropriate or unintelligible, then I will consider this undertaking to have been a failure - and it will need to be re-done.

Ever since I came across 'Adapa', I have had an unwavering belief that its story *and* its content - whatever may have been its original purpose - can be stimulating and of meaning to readers from all backgrounds. It may have different impact on each group of readers, but that is unavoidable. My job has been to try and make its text as living and vibrant as possible.

A central aim has been to use language that can be understood by everyone, although this has not prevented me from using rarer terms and less common turns of phrase wherever these were required. Words like 'afore', 'bethink' and 'aslumber' may not be used in everyday speech, but where an archaic or poetic word was more fitting than any other, I have gone ahead and used it. Perhaps, sometimes, my style of writing has bordered on the colloquial, but I have only done so when I felt that this was well-suited to the character speaking and not in any passages of narration. Whether my style of translation helps to bring the 'Adapa' text *to life* - which is my core purpose - I cannot know in advance, but I do hope that in spite of errors of inaccuracy (that I am **sure** I have made), this story will reach more readers than ever.

As for the *second* aim of this translation, by saying that I do not want "to limit it to one viewpoint alone", I mean that I did not want to compose this text in such a way that my version would limit 'Adapa' to solely *one interpretation*. After reading as widely as I could in the literature of 'Adapademia', I realized how damaging it would be to use words and phrases that might, in a narrow-minded fashion, restrict this translation to the perspectives of only one or other scholarly view - when it is possible that even at the time of the original *experience* of the text (be that as religious ritual, semi-dramatic enactment *etc.*), the audience may have had variable interpretations of the story, especially moving from one era to another.

Taking Enki's advice to Adapa, for example - I did not want to limit the text *only* to a view that Enki is deceiving Adapa, nor to a view that it is well-known that food and water of the Gods are toxic to humans, nor to any other *one* limited interpretation. *One of them* or *none of them* may be true, yet by using plain language that does not commit me to one or other theory of 'Adapa' alone, I hope that readers with differing points of view will be able to approach the text as they wish. Take, as another instance, the passage where Adapa's boat appears to have been capsized by the South Wind - there is no need to commit the text, one way or the other, to whether Adapa is still *alive*, already *dead*, or in a region somewhere *in between* life and death. Each time we read a text we can view things differently - personally, I am aware that I do this. I realized, in the light of numerous elucidations proposed about this text, that I wanted to be careful not to lock into any definitive view of the story and turn it into a 'closed text'. Instead, I have opted for a certain degree of ambiguity so as to allow for variant readings - thus giving to readers a greater freedom.

Arriving at the *third* and final key aim that I have tried to attain with this work of poetry, my goal has not been to translate a certain amount of sentences, or to just convert words from one language into another - but rather to manage to translate the 'Adapa' work as a whole from a group of source texts. If I were to have tackled this as a *purely linguistic task*, I would not have made progress. The only reason that I have succeeded in producing this work, is due to the immense wealth of well-evidenced, highly detailed research that has been invested into 'Adapa' — which has resulted in numerous crucial aspects of this critical text being 'unlocked' over the last century.

Without the solid analysis of the sources that has been so well-documented and debated, *I would not have been able to create this work.* I only apologize that - in order to prevent this work from getting any longer - I have not made annotated reference to the academic literature everywhere it is relied on. Like N.K. Sandars' work with 'Epic of Gilgamesh', I have been reliant on the work of others so as to achieve this task. Like hers also - although on a far smaller scale - I have attempted an artificial synthesis of a whole from its disparate parts. It is my highest hope that I have created some kind of experience of 'Adapa' that has not existed for readers previously - no 'definitive translation' yet one that is satisfying as a work of fiction in terms of drama and meaning.

At no point during the overly long process of translational composition, have I ceased to be aware that this is just the highly fallible product of a human being. However, *that was never going to stop being true,* so I have had to make my mind up to finish this work in a way which, even though it cannot satisfy everyone, is nonetheless the best that I am capable of. In order to complete this task, I have had to abandon 'perfectionism', for if I was to delay myself with the choice of each and every word till I was a hundred percent certain that it was perfect - I would never be able to arrive at the finalization of this composition. A quest for PERFECTION would have killed off *Adapa's Ascent* — I would not let that writer's malady crush me longer!

Right now, I have arrived at a point where there is nothing else to do but to let go of 'Adapa' and hope that he lets go of me too! Releasing this translation is the most difficult part of all, because I have to do so even though it is impossible for me to be entirely satisfied with what I have produced. However, as this task of 'Re-Creation' is at an end and there is no more that I can contribute to the text, it is the moment for me to let others peruse it and arrive at their own estimates of it as they will — *negative* or *positive*.

'Adapa' has been a companion of many years and even though that may sound strange, it really does feel as if I am leaving behind someone whom I have come to know well. His drama has been one that I thought about every day and this task simply refused to be left aside until it was completed. There is nothing more to say here about the composition or editing of this poetic translation, so it is time for me to bring this essay to an end. For those interested in how this author perceived the overall narrative and textual purpose of *Adapa's Ascent*, I would direct them to also read the essay *'The Birth of Fiction'* (which is included at the start of this volume). Apart from that, the only other thoughts I have to share about this work are at the end of this book — playfully speculative in nature — in the form of a casual essay titled 'Parting with Adapa'.

# C. THE SOURCES OF
## *ADAPA'S ASCENT*

THE PRESENT WORK - *Adapa's Ascent* - owes **everything** to the cuneiform sources from which it has been derived. These have been discussed in some detail within the preceding essay but it would be improper not to include representations of the tablets in some form. The current section provides photo reproductions of the entirety of cuneiform sources that have formed the basis of this translation. It is not possible - in a book of this size - to give lifesize photographs of any of the tablets and fragments, but nonetheless it is hoped that these pictures will adequately evidence the concrete realities upon which this English verse translation is based. The photos of the Amarna tablet and Nineveh fragments are those provided by Prof. Shlomo Izre'el in his book 'Adapa and the South Wind', while the images of the Tell Haddad tablets are those furnished by Prof. Antoine Cavigneaux in his article 'Une version sumérienne de la légende d'Adapa'. - I have used the letters applied by Prof. Izre'el to the former tablets (which are generally accepted as standard in Adapa scholarship) and although it is *not yet* common practice, I have labelled the Sumerian tablets as $S^1$, $S^2$, $S^3$ *etc.* so as to distinguish them from each other. Anyone interested in reading the cuneiform can refer to the two texts cited above, which include accurate diagrammatic illustrations of each of the tablets as well as transliterations of all the symbols.

Fragment A

Fragment A[1]

Fragment B (Obverse)

Fragment B (Reverse)

Fragment C

Fragment D

Fragment E (Obverse)

Fragment E (Reverse)

Tablet S[1]

Tablet S²

Tablet S³

Tablet S⁴

Tablet S⁵

Tablet S<sup>6</sup>

# D. TRANSLATION SKETCH
# OF A SUMERIAN TEXT

ONE OF THE MOST fascinating discoveries in recent
years is that of the Sumerian versions of the Adapa
myth. Dug up around forty years ago at Tell Haddad
(ancient Meturan) they have transformed the face of
'Adapa' scholarship. Two complete texts were excavated, though they are substantially similar except in
minor details. For the sake of simplicity I will refer
to them jointly as *one text*. Ever since first reading
Prof. Cavigneaux's French translation of the Sumerian text, I have been gripped by this early version of
the Adapa legend, with its very different focus and
broader narrative — though the core events of Adapa
cursing the South Wind, being given advice by Enki
and going to visit Anu in Heaven *etc.*, are the same.

From lines 101-190 of the Tell Haddad recension, we are presented with a critical, earlier version
of the 'Adapa' narrative, dating from circa 1760 BCE.
Also, over the previous hundred lines, we are provided
with a *prequel* to the 'Adapa' drama as we know it. This
earlier portion of the text presents the 'Adapa' (here
called 'Adaba') myth from after the reëstablishment of
humans on Earth following a Great Flood. Whereas
the sections of the text recounting the 'Adapa' narrative
(cursing the South Wind, being called to Heaven *etc.*)
are almost entirely intact, parts of the tablets recounting post-diluvian events are badly damaged in numerous areas, in some places are almost entirely illegible.

At several places in this book, I have referred to this earlier part of the Sumerian text as the 'Flood Prologue'. However, it is unlikely that it was ever referred to as a *prologue* - the text being continuous, with no distinct parts - and this lengthy stage of the Sumerian 'Adaba' text barely shares any details about a flood. What it describes, rather, is a period *directly following on from* the occurrence of an immense flood. Its focus is on *how the World was set up anew,* with '*Man*' in it, especially how the Gods and human beings accomplished this new phase of civilization together.

Reading through the fragments of the post-Flood narrative that *are* legible, it is noteworthy how many elements of it are common to a number of Sume-rian texts dating from the same period — above all to the 'Epic of Atrahasis', the 'Eridu Genesis' and a shorter text commonly entitled 'Rulers of Lagash'. The 'Atrahasis' text dates from the 17th Century BCE, while this Sumerian version of 'Adapa' dates back to the 18th Century. The 'Eridu Genesis' text, however - still the oldest existing account of a 'Great Flood' like in the 'Book of Genesis' - dates back as far as 2300 BCE, so it is possible its material was known to the authors of this version of 'Adapa'. As for the text on the 'Rulers of Lagash', it dates back to approximately the 21st Century BCE and has a number of phrases and vocabulary in common with *this* Sumerian text.

Looking at some damaged portions of the Tell Haddad recension of 'Adapa', it appears to me that a number of the gaps may be speculatively extrapolated with assistance from the three texts above, *inter alia*. It may be dangerous to fill in the spaces where it is not known what was written there, but I felt that it may not be without value to make an initial attempt at composing a 'Translation Sketch' of what the complete text *may have been,* while having no clue which guesswork is on the right tracks and which is thoroughly wrong. The gaps in the current Tell Haddad tablets, due to the serious damage they have suffered, makes it impossible to know exactly what is written there. The 'sketch' that follows makes no claims to being an accurate representation of the Sumerian text in English, being simply a preliminary attempt at creating a choate experience of an earlier stage in the telling of 'Adapa' — it is error-prone and flawed by nature, which is inevitable when forging a '*texte intégral*' from a source so disintegrated.

As author of this sketch, I owe the academic community deepest apologies for all errors that I have made. I am *thoroughly indebted* to the decipherment of the Sumerian tablets by Prof. Antoine Cavigneaux and his French translation of all recognizable symbols in the groundbreaking article 'Une version Sumérienne de la légende d'Adapa' (2014). I am also indebted to Prof. Amar Annus's independent analysis (and first translation into English) of the Sumerian 'Adapa' text in Appendix 1 of his illuminating study 'The Overturned Boat' (2016). His interpretations shed alternate light on many symbols and phrases occurring in the tablets, though it is still hard to decide whose exegesis is correct without a better preserved Sumerian version.

One of the many exciting aspects of the Tell Haddad version of 'Adapa' is that it presents itself as a complete narrative - far longer than the later versions - which has multiple key factors in common with those versions and other surviving fragments. It is interesting to see how the core chain of events - from Adapa cursing the South Wind to his refusing the Food and Water of Life - is *similar* (but not identical) across all versions. It is particularly fascinating to see certain small details (such as the joke about mourning the deaths of Dumuzi and Ningishzida) already present here. Most notable, however, is inclusion of an 'Invocation' at the end, which supports a view that the *origins* of the curative power of Adapa's very name is one key purpose of the narrative. It is especially significant that the Sumerian version of 'Adapa' was found in the library of an 'Exorcist' - a role with which this figure is increasingly identified (*qv.* Milstein, Annus et al.).

In contrast to the core poem '*Adapa's Ascent*' presented in this volume, the following 'sketch' has been formatted in a far plainer manner throughout, in a style that aims to be in keeping with the content and tenor of the text while not introducing any excessive verbal coloration or contrived linguistic devices. It is my hope that, in the not-too-distant future, the large lacunæ in the Sumerian text will be filled in - due to new research, analysis and fresh discoveries - so it will be possible for a *genuine translation* to be accomplished. Professors Cavigneaux and Annus are not responsible for any of the liberties I took with this poem. — All errors are my own.

# ADAPA's ASCENT
## AFTER THE FLOOD

*AND IN THOSE distant days*
*when Earth and Sky had been reborn,*

*And in those distant nights -*
*those nights elapsed so endless past,*

*And in those distant years,*
*those years from memory*
*so long passed . . .*

— After the floods had
burst forth from the skies and
had led all the country to utter disaster;
after mankind had been ground into dust
and all of the land - north to south
- had been razed to the ground,

none of the HOLY GODS
had *a place on this Earth*
to eat or drink - THEIR Temples
had not been founded and no-one
has toiled to make THEM bread!

- though AN and ENLIL , ENKI
and NINHURSAGA saw to it
the seed of humankind,
*it had been salvaged.*

Once *New Creation* - from
what had survived of the land
of the dark-headed people -
had been accomplished,

all of the four-legged creatures
roamed far and wide over the country.
In thickets dense with giant grass and
in the ponds, and in the reed-beds,
fishes and birds of every kind
- they multiplied in number.

High upon the plateaus,
herbs aromatic and plants
grew rich and lush and fruitful.
Then there was no need to share
mere canals - for their sources,
those mighty twin rivers,
the *Tigris, Euphrates,*
were *LIFE OF THE LAND.*

Then the *Wise One*
made sure that the earth
was tilled, the ground cleared,
channels dug to provide people
water - canals with levees, streams
flowing everywhere — Enki, *yes,*
he helped humanity find
their way again.

Food and drink were
abundant and plenty as
AN and ENLIL put order
back into this world —

they created
the town of Kish
that pillar of the nation,
then the chosen shepherd,
Etana - so greatly renowned
for his words and deeds -
became monarch and
guide to mankind.

A dynasty royal would be
founded. He who began in
a pasture - grazing his sheep in
the fields - the King became with
regal palace, pulled in his chariot
in procession. The state of man
did not concern him — *All in
his Kingdom seemed good.*

The SOUTH WIND - Etana
upon the throne - *She blessed
the land.* She did not breathe
nor with anger nor hatred.

— But humanity had not
been given a true direction.
Gods' servants, no guidance
had they been provided. —
*He was not told **where to go**.*
*He was not told **what to do** -*
The LORD had not designated
roles or delegated tasks.

*"Man does things as he sees fit"*,
he progresses without any order
- the LORD became weakened by
this, then HE lay himself down.
Knowing what had to be said,
HE spoke to the people as one
— HIS instructions HE gave
with WORDS OF LIGHT :

*"To the ends of the Earth*
*you made animals graze —*
*now may you be **just as wise***
*to preserve your grain in stores.*
*- For **you people** knew how to sow*
*seeds to grow. Once the winds have*
*breathed vapors of LIFE upon them,*
*— gather together your bounty!*

*The WIND of the NORTH,*
*WIND of STORM and DISASTER -*
*will you save harvests from HIM ?*
*For ASHNAN, HE passed back and forth*
*across fields that reached horizonwide,*
*separating ears from the chaff while*
*SHULLAT and HANISH reaped barley*
*sweet and fresh for the people. "*

Humanity is in disarray, they
have no set course or direction -
some times bring them death and yet
others bring wealth - though each one of
their lives *the LORD ordains with* **Destiny.**
People save sustenance for themselves
but *YOU* it is who gives them breath
= *YOU GIVE HUMANITY LIFE* =

YOU touched the lips of *man*
and YOU gave *him* the power of
SPEECH. YOU fashioned *his being*
according to YOUR OWN. — YOU gave
YOUR intelligence — IT BECAME HIS OWN.
To help mankind get along in the World,
YOU gave them wisdom : *YOU showed*
*the fisherman* **how to catch fish** *! "*

- With his adeptness,
Adapa gave sweet barley
to the people - he gave life to
the land by digging and clearing
canals that watered every plot.
He cultivated countless crops
till they all grew a-plenty.

*Truly, it was magnificent.*
*Truly, it was great.*

The vast fields were
abounding with crops.
The rivers were crowded
with fishes, with birds - sugar
plantations burst with sweetness:
"*My LORD, for YOU I fish carp*
*in the waters. For YOU*
*I do all to please.*"

But then, UPON THAT
DAY - at the Holy Port,
*Harbour of the New Moon*
- did Adapa board his boat and
set sail. His vessel, without any
oars or rudder, it drifted along
with the flow of the current.

— Upon the vast lake
where he came out to fish,
Adapa cast his nets to catch
carp for the House of his LORD.
For the galleries and halls of
ENKI's inner sanctum he was
catching fish, to bestow
as *sacred offerings*.

On the great twin rivers
- Euphrates and Tigris -
the SOUTH WIND raised up
her most powerful storms,
but Adapa - son of Eridu - he
did curse that SOUTH WIND !
*Did he know where **those**
**words** would lead him?*

With his curse, he had severed
the wings of the SOUTH WIND.

*— For seven whole days and
for seven whole nights did
the SOUTH WIND blow not
on the Land.* And so did
AN the Great - Divine -
his vizier Kagia address:

"Come now, my dearest
companion in dialogue
- Kagia, my vizier loyal -
so consummately skilled :
why for seven whole days
and seven whole nights
has the South Wind not
blown upon the land ? "

Kagia responded to
AN, King of the Gods :
"It was Adapa, my LORD,
- he known as the Sage -
of Eridu, Guardian.

At the Holy Harbour
- **Port of the New Moon** -
he got aboard his sea-boat,

then he set sail and his vessel,
without any oars or rudder,
it drifted along with
the water's flow.
Upon the vast lake
where he came to fish,
Adapa cast his nets to catch
carp for the House of his LORD.

*For the galleries and halls of
the Temple of ENKI he was
gathering fish to provide
as his holy offerings. —
On the great twin rivers
- Euphrates and Tigris -
the SOUTH WIND raised up
HER most powerful storms.*

*But Adapa - son of Eridu -*
**he cursed that SOUTH WIND.**
*Little he knew where those
words would lead him. —*

*With his curse he had severed
the wings of the SOUTH WIND
- then over the lands did
the wind cease to blow."*

AN, he spoke some words
to Kagia - scarcely had these
left his mouth than did Kagia,
by herald, convey them to Adapa :

*"AN - King of the GODS - addresses
HIMSELF to Adapa, the Sage, and
he orders him* — **You must present
yourself <u>NOW</u>** *in the presence of AN."*

Then ENKI addressed HIMSELF
to Adapa, giving instruction
to him with these words:

"*Adapa — you will
ascend to the FATHER.
Do not have fear of HIM.
Do not accept...*

*When HE offers you
bread to eat -* **do not say 'Yes'.**
*When HE offers you
water to drink -* **do not say 'Yes'.**
*Bread and water are
gifts of mortality -
as HE offers them to you
— YOU MUST NOT ACCEPT THEM!*

*When He offers to you a robe
-* **do not take it from HIM.** *But
when HE offers you ointment
-* **cover your body with this.**

*Adapa, you must wear
your hair dishevelled
— let it be crawling
with loathsome lice.*

*- Two GODS who are there
shall approach you: DUMUZI
and NINGISHZIDA. THEY will
ask of you then: 'Young man,
why are you wearing your hair
like this?' - You will answer THEM
thus: 'In our town two GODS have
died - that is why I appear to YOU so.*

*Lord DUMUZI and Lord NINGISHZIDA
have died - and so I appear to You thus'.*

They will look into each other's eyes
*- and at this will They smile.*

Adapa, he took to heart
the directions of his MASTER.
He wore his hair loose and he let
it become so infested with lice.

With UTU he entered
the base of the Heavens
- with UTU was Adapa led
to AN's Heavenly Gates.
He was led all the way
to the Palace of AN,
to the FATHER of
All the GODS.

Two GODS who were there
approached Adapa - DUMUZI
and NINGISHZIDA - and THEY
asked him then: *'Young Man,*
*why are you wearing your hair*
*in mourning?'* He answered THEM
thus: *'In our town two GODS have*
*died - that is why I appear to YOU so.*

*Lord DUMUZI and Lord NINGISHZIDA*
*have died - and so I appear to YOU thus.'*

— THEY looked into each other's eyes
*and at this did THEY smile.*

"Adapa, he has paid
close attention to
the instructions
of Lord ENKI."

**On the day of Great Light,**
**upon the day of Cleansing,**
**on the day of the New Moon,**
**upon the day of Judgments —**
The GODS presented Adapa to AN,
*while in a good mood.* AN gave Adapa
(Wise One, of Great Understanding)
a seat as a sign of being welcomed.

When AN offered Adapa
bread to eat - **he refused it**.
When AN offered Adapa
water to drink - **he refused it**.
When he was brought a garment
to wear - **he rejected it as well**.
When he was offered an ointment
- **he covered his body with it**.

AN said to Adapa: *"Eat! Drink!"*
and He laughed at him then.

*"Father ENKI,*
*in making him*
*act as one bereaved*
*- his face sick with grief -*
*has stopped ME from giving*
*MY Gift of Life to him!"*

- And after that AN,
within the Assembly,
addressed HIS words
to the GREAT GODS:

*"Adapa - why did he break off*
*the wings of the SOUTH WIND?"*

And the GREAT GODS
responded to AN:

"*ENKI must see to it now that*
*the wings of the SOUTH WIND*
*are fixed - that the SOUTH WIND*
*shall blow as SHE should once again.*

*Through devoting HIS time and*
*attention to this - ENKI must then*
*see that* **henceforth** *the Edicts, Rules*
*and Law of AN will be kept in the land.*"

ENKI addressed Himself
then to the SOUTH WIND:

"*Come SOUTH WIND —* **now**
**I am going to set things right!**"

\*      \*      \*      \*      \*

Upon the high steppes in
the Place of Silence,
a man who is ill
- he will pray
in this way:

"My LORD, Your
blessed inscription will
make sure the SOUTH WIND's
breath does not touch my body.
On the expanses of the vast lakes,
illness will not flow through
the waters, but pass away,
causing no-one illness".

- It shall be defeated
by these Holy Words:

"Illness and ailments
attacking my human body,
- may Breath of the SOUTH WIND
remove them all from me!

For the dressings of Holy NINSINA
(which have soothed my suffering)
GREAT PRINCE OF THE GODS - FATHER
ENKI - HALLOWED BE THY NAME!"

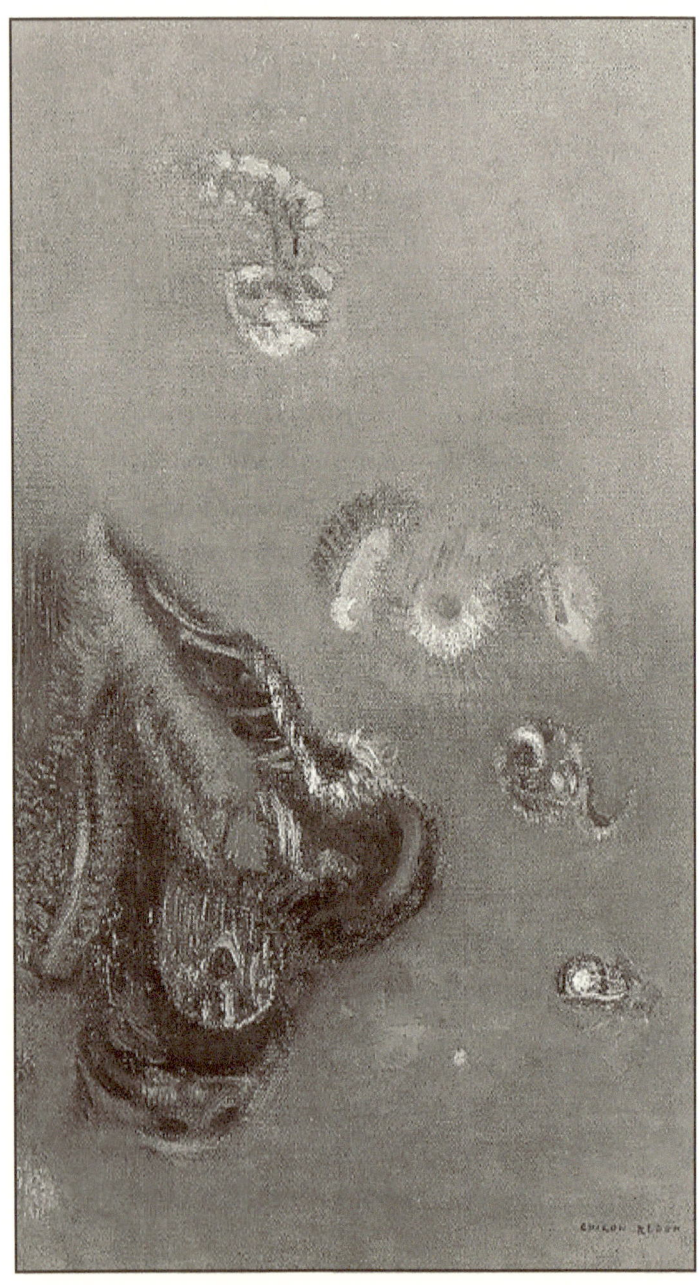

# E. SUGGESTIONS FOR
# FURTHER READING

I HAVE NOT NAMED this a 'bibliography' as it is no more than a list of *suggestions* for further reading. It may interest those who wish to learn more about the 'Adapa' myth and interpretation of the narrative. It includes some translations and research works that have been referred to during the composition process. The books and articles mentioned below are listed in chronological and not alphabetical order. For the sake of brevity - and as this is not an academic publication - I have provided the minimum information possible in order to assist any curious researchers in finding these books and articles in print and online. Publication names are written in italics and names of articles are written in standard text. In some instances, to assist in locating a contribution referred to, I have specified the page numbers in the volume as well.

*The Chaldean Account of Genesis. Containing the Description of the Creation, the Fall of Man, the Deluge, the Tower of Babel, the Times of the Patriarchs, and Nimrod; Babylonian Fables, and Legends of the Gods; from the Cuneiform Inscriptions* (1876) George **Smith**

*A Catalogue of the Cuneiform Tablets in the Kouyunjik Collection of the British Museum* [5 Vols.] (1889-99) C. **Bézold**

*The Golden Bough: A Study in Comparative Religion* [2 Vols.] (1890) James George **Frazer**

The Babylonian Legend of the Creation of Man. *The Academy* 1055 [July 23, 1892] p.72 (1892) Archibald H. **Sayce**

Note on a Fragment of the Adapa Legend. *Proceedings of the Society of Biblical Archaeology* 16 pp.274-279 (1894) S. Arthur **Strong**

Die babylonischen Legenden von Etana, Zu, Adapa und Dibarra [The Babylonian Legends of Etana, Zu, Adapa and Dibarra]. *Beiträge zur Assyriologie und semitischen Sprachwissenschaft* 2 pp.390-521 (1894) Edward T. **Harper**

Additional Note on a Fragment of the Adapa Legend. *Proceedings of the Society of Biblical Archeology* 17 p.44 (1895) S. Arthur **Strong**

*Cuneiform Parallels to the Old Testament* (1912) Robert William **Rogers**

*Four Stages of Greek Religion: Studies Based on a Course of Lectures Delivered in April 1912 at Columbia University* (1912) Gilbert **Murray**

*A Hebrew Deluge Story in Cuneiform and Other Epic Fragments in the Pierpont Morgan Library* (1922) Albert T. **Clay** [republished as *Atrahasis: An Ancient Hebrew Deluge Story* (2003)]

Ea-Mummu and Anu-Adapa in the Panegyric of Cyrus. *Journal of the Royal Asiatic Society* pp.285-291 (1926) W.F. **Albright**

*Beowulf: A Translation and Commentary* (1926) J.R.R. **Tolkien** [Published 2014; Ed. C. **Tolkien**]

*The Decline of the West* [2 Vols.] (1918) Oswald **Spengler** [Translation: Charles F. **Atkinson** (1926)]

A Note on Adapa. *Orientalia* (old series) 30 p.24 (1928) E. **Burrows**

Il Mito di Adapa [The Myth of Adapa]. *Reconditi della R. Accademia Nazionale dei Lincei, Classe di Scienza Morali, Storische e Filologiche* 6/5 pp.113-171 (1929) Giuseppe **Furlani**

The Investiture and Anointing of Adapa in Heaven. *American Journal of Semitic Languages and Literatures* 46 pp.201-203 (1929-30) Thorkild **Jacobsen**

*The Epic of Gilgamesh: Text, Transliteration and Notes* (1930) R. **Campbell Thompson**

*The Odyssey* by **Homer** [Translation from the Greek by Emile Victor **Rieu** (1946)]

*Before Philosophy: The Intellectual Adventure of Ancient Man* (1949) Henri **Frankfort**, Mrs. H.A. **Frankfort**, John A. **Wilson** & Thorkild **Jacobsen**

*The Hero with a Thousand Faces* (1949) Joseph J. **Campbell**

Adapa. *Ancient Near-Eastern Texts Relating to the Old Testament* [Ed. J.B. **Pritchard**] pp.101-103 (1950) Ephraim A. **Speiser**

*The Pyramid Texts* (1952) [Translation from the Original Hieroglyphs] Samuel A. B. **Mercer**

*The Outline of History - The Whole Story of Man* [*qv.* Book III, Chapter 13 - 'The Early Empires'] (1956) Herbert George **Wells**

Die Mythe vom weisen Adapa [The Myth of Adapa the Wise]. *Die Welt des Orients* 2 pp.416-431 (1959) Franz Marius Theodor de Liagre **Böhl**

*The Epic of Gilgamesh* (1960) Nancy K. **Sandars**

*Alpha and Omega: A Study in the Pattern of Revelation* [pp.7-11] (1961) Samuel Henry **Hooke**

Adapa, le vent et l'eau. *Revue d'Assyriologie* 55 pp.13-33 (1961) Georges **Roux**

The Etiological Myth of the Seven Sages. *Orientalia* 30 pp.1-11 (1961) Erica **Reiner**

On the Antiquity of Sumerian Literature. *Journal of the American Oriental Society* 83 pp.167-176 (1963) William W. **Hallo**

*Middle Eastern Mythology* (1963) S.H. **Hooke**

*Mesopotamien: Die Mythologie der Sumerer und Akkader* [Mesopotamians: The Mythology of the Sumerians and the Akkadians] (1965) Dietz Otto **Edzard**

***Atra-Ḫasīs,** The Babylonian Story of the Flood* (1969) W.G. **Lambert** & A.R. **Millard**

*Les Religions du Proche-Orient Asiatique: Textes Babyloniens, Ougaritiques, Hittites* [Religions of the Middle East: Babylonian, Ugaritic and Hittite texts] (1970) René **Labat** *et al.*

*Poems of Heaven and Hell from Ancient Mesopotamia* (1971) Nancy K. **Sandars** [qv. ʿAdapa the Manʾ pp.167-172]

*The Epic* (1971) Paul **Merchant**

L'inganno di Ea nel mito di Adapa [Ea's Deceit in the Myth of Adapa]. *Oriens Antiquus* 12 pp.257-266 (1973) - P. **Xella**

Adapa, Genesis and the Notion of Faith. *Ugarit Forschungen* 5 pp.61-66 (1973) Giorgio **Buccellati**

Die Weisheit des Adapa von Eridu [The Wisdom of Adapa of Eridu]. *Symbolæ Biblicæ et Mesopotamicæ Francisco Mario Theodoro de Liagre Böhl Dedicatæ* pp.234-239 (1973) Burkhart **Kienast**

Wisdom and Gods in Ancient Mesopotamia. *Orientalia* 43 pp.344-354 (1974) Benjamin **Foster**

Ein Adapa Fragment aus Ninive [An Adapa Fragment from Nineveh] *Orientalia* 43 pp.162-164 (1974) W. **Schramm**

Studies in Sumerian Proverbs. *Mesopotamia: Copenhagen Studies in Assyriology* 3 (1975) Bendt **Alster**

Bemerkungen zum Adapa-Mythos [Observations on the Myth of Adapa] *Kramer Anniversary Volume. Cuneiform Studies in Honor of Samuel Noah Kramer* [Ed. B. **Eichler**] *Alter Orient und Altes Testament* 25 pp.427-433 (1976) Wolfram **von Soden**

*The Babyloniaca of Berossus* (1978) Stanley Mayer **Burstein**

Adapa and the Ritual Process. *Rocznik Orientalistyczny* 41 pp.77-82 (1980) Piotr **Michałowski**

*Il Poemetto di Adapa* [The Poem of Adapa] (1981) Sergio Angelo **Picchioni**

Adam and Adapa: Two Anthropological Characters. *Andrews University Seminary Studies* 19 pp.179-194 (1981) Niels-Erik **Andreason**

*The Unbearable Lightness of Being* (1984) Milan Kundera [Translation: Michael Henry **Heim**]

Mythos als Gattung archäischen Erzählens und die Geschichte von Adapa [Myth as archaic mode of storytelling and the story of Adapa]. *Archiv für Orientforschung* 29-30 pp.75-89 (1984) Hans-Peter **Müller**

Adapa and Humanity: Mortal or Evil? *Journal of the Ancient Near Eastern Society* 18 pp.1-2 (1986) J.D. **Bing**

Literatur: Überblick über die akkadische Literatur [Literature: An Overview of the Akkadian Literature]. *Reallexikon der Assyriologie* 7 pp.48-66 (1987) W. **Röllig**

*Myths of Enki, the Crafty God* (1989) Samuel Noah **Kramer** & John **Maier**

*Myths from Mesopotamia: Creation, the Flood, Gilgamesh and Others* (1989) Stephanie **Dalley**

*Mesopotamian Myths: The Legendary Past* (1990) Henrietta **McCall**

Le Mythe d'Adapa [The Myth of Adapa]. *Studi Epigrafici e Linguistici sul Vicino Oriente Antico* 7 pp.43-57 (1990) Philippe **Talon**

Wurde Adapa um das Ewige Leben betrogen? [Was Adapa cheated of Eternal Life?]. *Mitteilung für Anthropologie und Religionsgeschichte* 6 pp.119-132 (1991) Manfried **Dietrich**

See Red: Reflections on the Amarna Recension of Adapa. *Semitic Studies in Honor of Wolf Leslau on the Occasion of his 85ᵗʰ Birthday,* Vol. 1 [Ed. Alan S. Kaye] pp.746-772 (1991) Shlomo **Izre'el**

*Babylonian Literary Tests from Western Libraries* (1993) Manfried **Dietrich**

The Study of Oral Poetry: Reflections of a Neophyte. *Mesopotamian Epic Literature: Oral or Aural?* (Eds: M.E. **Vogelzang** & H.L.J. **Vanstiphout**) pp.155-225 (1993) Shlomo **Izre'el**

*Before the Muses: An Anthology of Akkadian Literature* [2 Vols.] (1993) Benjamin R. **Foster**

New Readings in the Amarna Versions of Adapa and Nergal and Ereškigal (1993) *Journal of the Institute of Archaeology of Tel Aviv University, Occasional Publications* 1 pp.51-67 (1993) Shlomo **Izre'el**

New Literary Texts from Tell Haddad (Ancient Meturan): A First Survey. *Iraq* 55 pp.91-101 (1993) Antoine **Cavigneaux** & Farouk **Al-Rawi**

Did Adapa Indeed Lose His Chance for Eternal Life? *Target* 6 pp.15-41 (1994) Shlomo **Izre'el**

*From Distant Days: Myths, Tales, and Poetry of Ancient Mesopotamia* [2 Vols.] (1995) Benjamin R. **Foster** [Abridged 1-Vol. Edition published 2018]

Mesopotamian Myth in Contemporary Setting: Translating Akkadian Myths. *Mesopotamian Poetic Language: Sumerian and Akkadian* (Editors: M.E. **Vogelzang** & H.L.J. **Vanstiphout**) pp.85-125 (1996) Shlomo **Izre'el** [includes the 'Verse Translation of Adapa' by Anne **Kilmer** pp.111-123]

The Initiation of Adapa into Heaven. *Intellectual Life of the Ancient Near East: Papers Presented at the 43ʳᵈ Rencontre Assyriologique Internationale, Prague.* pp.183-187 (1996) Shlomo **Izre'el**

*The Amarna Scholarly Tablets* (1997) Shlomo **Izre'el**

*šimâ milka: Induktion und Reception der mittelbabylonischen Dichtung von Ugarit, Emar und Tell el-Amarna* [šimâ milka: Induction and Reception of Middle Babylonian Poetry from Ugarit, Emar and Tell el-Amarna] (1998) Thomas R. **Kämerer**

A Scholar's Library in Meturan. With an Edition of the Tablet H 72. *Textes de Tell Haddad 7* (1999) Antoine **Cavigneaux**

*Adapa and the South Wind: Language has the Power of Life and Death* (2001) Shlomo **Izre'el**

Adapa o la immortalidad frustrada. Reflexiones sobre el poema de Adapa [Adapa, or Immortality frustrated. Reflections on the poem of Adapa]. *Isimu* VIII pp.173-200 (2005) Rafael Jimenez **Zamudio**

*Superheroes and Gods: A Comparative Study from Babylonia to Batman* (2007) Don **LoCicero**

The Four Winds and the Origins of Pazuzu. *Das geistige Erfassen der Welt im Alten Orient. Beiträge zu Sprache, Religion, Kultur und Gesellschaft* [Ed. C. Wilcke *et alia*] pp.125-165 (2007) Frans A.M. **Wiggermann**

*Storytelling: An Encyclopædia of Mythology and Folklore* (2008) Josepha Sherman

Another Wrinkle on Old Adapa. *Studies in Ancient Near Eastern World View and Society presented to Marten Stol on the occasion of his 65th Birthday* [Ed. R.J. van der Spek *et al.*] pp.1-10 (2008) Jack M. **Sasson**

*Primeval History: Babylonian, Biblical and Enochic - An Intertextual Reading* (2011) Helge S. **Kvanvig**

Une Version Sumérienne de la Légende d'Adapa [A Sumerian Version of the Adapa Legend]. *Zeitschrift für Assyriologie und vorderasiatische Archäologie* 104 (1) pp.1-41 (2014) Antoine **Cavigneaux**

Do Deities Deceive? *Windows to the Ancient World of the Hebrew Bible. Essays in Honor of Samuel Greengus* [Editors: B.T. **Arnold**, Nancy **Erickson**, & J.H. **Walton**] pp.201-214 (2014) Ronald **Veenker**

The Origins of Adapa. *Zeitschrift für Assyriologie* 105 (1) pp.30–41 (2015) Sara J. **Milstein**

The "Magic" of Adapa. *Texts and Contexts: Textual Transmission in the Cuneiform World* [Eds. Paul Delnero & Jacob Lauinger] pp.191-213 (2015) Sara J. **Milstein**

*The Overturned Boat: Intertextuality of the Adapa Myth and Exorcist Literature* (2016) Amar **Annus**

*Tracking the Master Scribe. Revision Through Introduction in Biblical and Mesopotamian Literature* (2016) Sara J. **Milstein**

A Middle Babylonian Sumerian Fragment of the Adapa Myth from Nippur and an Overview of the Middle Babylonian Sumerian Literary Corpus at Nippur. *The First Ninety Years: A Sumerian Celebration in Honor of Miguel Civil.* pp.255-276 (2017) Jeremiah **Peterson**

*From Adapa to Enoch: Scribal Culture and Religious Vision in Judea and Babylonia* [Texts and Studies in Ancient Judaism, Book 167] (2017) Seth L. **Sanders**

Marvel meets Mesopotamia: how modern comics preserve ancient myths @ *theconversation.com* (2018) Louise **Pryke**

\*      \*      \*      \*      \*

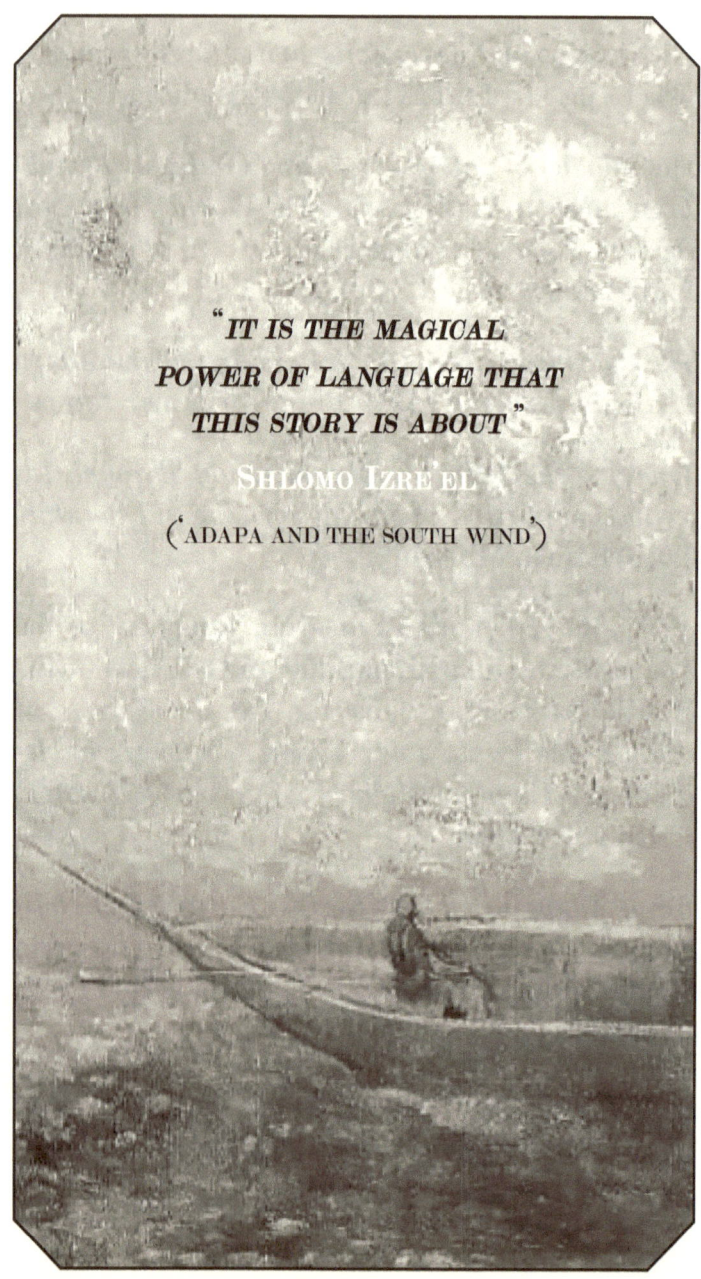

*"IT IS THE MAGICAL POWER OF LANGUAGE THAT THIS STORY IS ABOUT"*

SHLOMO IZRE'EL

('ADAPA AND THE SOUTH WIND')

# F. PARTING WITH ADAPA

I CAME TO THIS TASK like a Mesopotamian whose country no longer exists. I imagined that I were one of *those* people, living *then* — in fact, I imagined myself to be several of them, even to be Adapa himself. I know it sounds crazy, but *getting inside the mind of Adapa*, as far as this was even possible through the texts handed down, was what made a difference in writing.

I knew it would be impossible, living dozens of centuries after the original texts, to duplicate what was produced back then. Knowing that, my decision was to create something brand new which, though it may be as different from its sources as chalk from cheese, nonetheless might provide the reading public with something of value in itself. Whether I have achieved this, I will probably only know much later, or never.

The oft-quoted words of 15th century English poet John Lydgate are always relevant to the writer, whether of fiction, poetry, non-fiction or translation: "*You can please some of the people all of the time, you can please all of the people some of the time, but you can't please all of the people all of the time*". It may be that it is possible to reach wider publics with *Adapa's Ascent* than have been aware of that myth previously, but it is also inevitable that I will invoke the ire of *some* academics, due to the liberties I have taken with the text. However, I fear that if I wrote this work primarily for scholars, it would end up being more esoteric, and incapable of reaching general readers. —

The conclusion that I have arrived at is that I have to accept that I am going to disappoint everyone in some way or other with this book: there's no avoiding this.

Whether or not any further words about how I have approached this work are necessary, I personally need to voice several reflections as I wind down from composing this peculiar book. And I say "peculiar", because it is a strange combination of elements for me — fiction and poetry, non-fiction and translation: I have never been involved with a work anything like it before, and I doubt that I will ever do so again.

I KNEW THIS WAS GOING TO BE a time-consuming and multi-textured task when I set out - *at the outset.* My decision was that, if it were going to devour the flesh of my time, then I ought to commit myself all the way, in each of the areas or work required. Thus, I have invested it with the fullest efforts of my imagination and reason. True, I have been at a disadvantage in writing this work as an 'amateur', yet I set all my rational abilities to work - linguistic understanding, textual analysis, narrative logic *etc.* - while I released my creative faculties to the composition of its poetry.

To start with - predominantly due to my wider ignorance of Mesopotamia - I chose to restrict myself solely to the 'Adapa' texts in terms of my research. Though it is true I also spent time with 'Gilgamesh' translations for comparison, that general researches into that era of human civilization have been helpful, I have *only* read up deeply in areas directly relating to *this text* - meaning 'Adapa' scholarship exclusively, not academic writing on Sumerian and Akkadian fiction in general. Varying interpretations of all symbols on the tablets, new inputs from anthropology, emerging appreciation of ancient rituals: all these and more have been invaluable in assisting my guesswork (where required) by providing a better understanding of the cultural backdrops against which 'Adapa' texts emerged.

Although, on the one hand, it may be considered a shortcoming that I have restricted myself to Adapa-related scholarship alone in the process of composing this translation — for my part, it has been an integrated component of the 'method' approach I adopted throughout the course of writing it. I tried to *immerse myself* in the 'Adapa' texts, the religious practices of Sumerian and Akkadian societies, their perspectives on the Gods and the meaning of life, *for them* - all this helped me to put myself in the frame of mind of the story's scribes (or editors), the central characters (*viz.* Adapa, Enki, Anu), even that of the 'exorcist priests'.

What most caught my attention, in terms of the 'Incarnation Priest', is that each really practised something similar to a 'method' approach himself (whether there were 'incarnation priestesses' is unknown), for he would put himself entirely into a state of believing that *he was the person of Adapa* during the ritual, so that it *was Adapa himself who was relieving persons of all evils, illnesses, demonic possessions.* Visualizing the first person viewpoint of Adapa, as also of the Gods (Enki, Anu, Ninlil *etc.*), has been fundamental to the approach I have taken in creating this version of the narrative. I have done my best to get *inside* the story - not remain external to it.

Some may take issue with this approach to the translation, but in my opinion, it has enabled me more deeply to appreciate the viewpoints and attitudes of the protagonists and antagonists, thereby able to evaluate the inner rationale of varying interpretations of the sources. There are such a multiplicity of theories that have been written up about the meaning of different passages and incidents that I decided it would not be amiss to employ any means necessary in order to venture towards my own conclusions on a variety of topics. Where before it felt like I was just skating on the surface, confused about what *modus operandi* to adopt - in the case of the episodes in Heaven, for instance - through submerging myself deep into the drama and considering the different characters' points-of-view, I was able to make my mind up between differing explanations of scholars, often at odds with each other.

What I will say is that when the translator - as individual - believes that s/he has gained insight into the meanings behind words and the events that they portray, it is often possible s/he may have become blinded to other possibilities by the vibrancy of their own 'leading ideas'. In order to try and produce something that is not a mere transliteration of words or symbols, but something more - living, real, ideally a work of art in its own right - a translator must balance conviction in their own imaginational vision with open-minded appreciation of varying views, of other trans-lators, scholars — their contributions and solutions.

'Great Literature' presents us with themes and concerns that are of enduring value to humankind and that will likely continue to fascinate future genera-tions. It does not mean that there needs to have been a *realization* at the time the work was written, that it would be 'great' in future. Works that have passed the test of time are a miscellany of oddities and opposites - no matching set of plates and bowls, all created in conformity. What material similarities can be found between Plato's 'Dialogues', Dante's 'Divine Comedy', Shakespeare's Plays and Immanuel Kant's 'Critique of Pure Reason'? All that can be said is that *they will not go away* — they persist in their value and continue to be read because they excite curiosity, stimulate the senses, instigate original thinking, and more. '*Adapa's Ascent*', in my opinion (and I am sure to be biased be-cause I have spent far too long with this text) is a work of authentic value, likely to retain its '*classic*' status for many hundreds, if not thousands, more years to come.

What I have been continuously reminding my-self of while approaching 'Adapa' from the perspective of being a *modern-day translator*, is that my own view-points *can be nothing like* those from which Sumeri-ans, Akkadians, Assyrians, Babylonians, Egypt-ians and others viewed 'Adapa' in their own time. As one who is approaching the cuneiform remnants that have been left behind, from the point-of-view of *life in the 3rd Millennium CE*, how can I appreciate even a single one of the viewpoints of *those living in the 1st to 3rd Millennia BCE,* for whom 'Adapa' really mattered?

As I arrive at the final pages of this book, my mind is starting to see the myth of 'Adapa' in different ways than when I set out. Even though each part of the story is open to multiple interpretations, I now find myself unable to choose which of the possi-bilities I favor. Instead, as I re-read the text now, I find myself shifting between the varying outlooks on the narrative and its characters. I try to view 'Adapa' from the standpoints of different members of the audience. No single viewpoint is absolute — what problem is there with seeing a work from differing viewpoints? This general decision of mine, not to 'lock down' the work and confine it within any one specific interpretative view, but to try and embrace variant views as I re-read it, comes from spending perhaps too much time with the core sources — which, between them, leave count-less doors flung open to ambiguities and conflictions.

Regarding *Adapa* himself - as a figure - even though bold and striking vocabulary has been used to describe his actions and words, the episodes that occur leave his inner being (for the most part) in the dark. I think that what increases our interest in the **true he-roes** of fiction, is that we *never fully understand them,* nor *what makes them think and act as they do.* If we did, they would perhaps become emptier, transparent to us, and we could know in advance every action that they will take. With genuinely intriguing heroes of fic-tion, there is a suspense of action that derives from our not knowing quite exactly what the hero will do in the specific situations with which they are confronted. — What will Odysseus do with Penelope's suitors once he returns home from the longest journey? - What will occur after in Jason's life after he recovers the Golden Fleece? — No-one could perfectly predict what actions will be taken in these storylines, though we naturally envisage possible scenarios as we advance through a dramatic plot, visualizing the heroes' alternatives. The invisibility of Adapa's inner being increases the elements of unpredictability in the plot.

I do wish to reiterate here that the poetic translation I place before you is purely my own personal interpretation of the materials. Nonetheless, it *is* my sincere hope that some decisions made in this translational process will motivate further developments in the appreciation and the *continued translation* of this 'epic in miniature'. I stand by the view that, even though it is an exceedingly short work, 'Adapa' is an enduring one, in all eras deserving of readers. 'Smells like Teen Spirit' may only last four and a half minutes, yet in it *Nirvana* epitomized an entire generation — the 'Adapa' myth is equally compact in form, yet it may be the clearest distillation of the Mesopotamian World's overall view of humanity and Immortality.

Though I generally consider 'perfectionism' as the enemy - finding it so often impedes progress - there is one way in which I *have aimed* for this translation to be 'perfect'. As per the original form of the latin word '*perfectus*', perfect does not need to mean "flawless" but, in its primary meaning, "complete[d]". It has been my preliminary aim - in the creation of this version of 'Adapa' from a multiplicity of sources - to forge something that is *complete*. Insofar as I have managed to create a unified narrative from disparate, *incomplete sources*, I hope that I have, to some degree, been able to achieve that objective. All the while, I consider it still open to debate whether it is really is beneficial to produce a rounded work from materials which are by their nature so fragmentary — *imperfect*.

The truth is I have no idea whether this experiment - which is all I consider it - has been a success or a failure. Have I plunged into a precipice of error? Am I far beneath the waves like Adapa? I am unable to judge because - as I have admitted already - I have spent too long in isolation with 'Adapa' to retain an objective viewpoint any longer. *Adapa's Ascent*, the poem itself, has become like an old friend whose behaviors and mannerisms, even faults and eccentricities, I have come to accept over time. Those who approach this work afresh are likely to have a far more balanced viewpoint, coming to this book with the advantage of *new eyes* — able to see it *in their own personal light*.

My hope, in sending this book out from shore, is that it will introduce you to a drama of which you were never aware before: that reading 'Adapa's Ascent' will inspire you as much as it has inspired me, translating it. — *May YOU discover the mysteries of Adapa, whose name still echoes down the corridors of Time* —

**THE END**

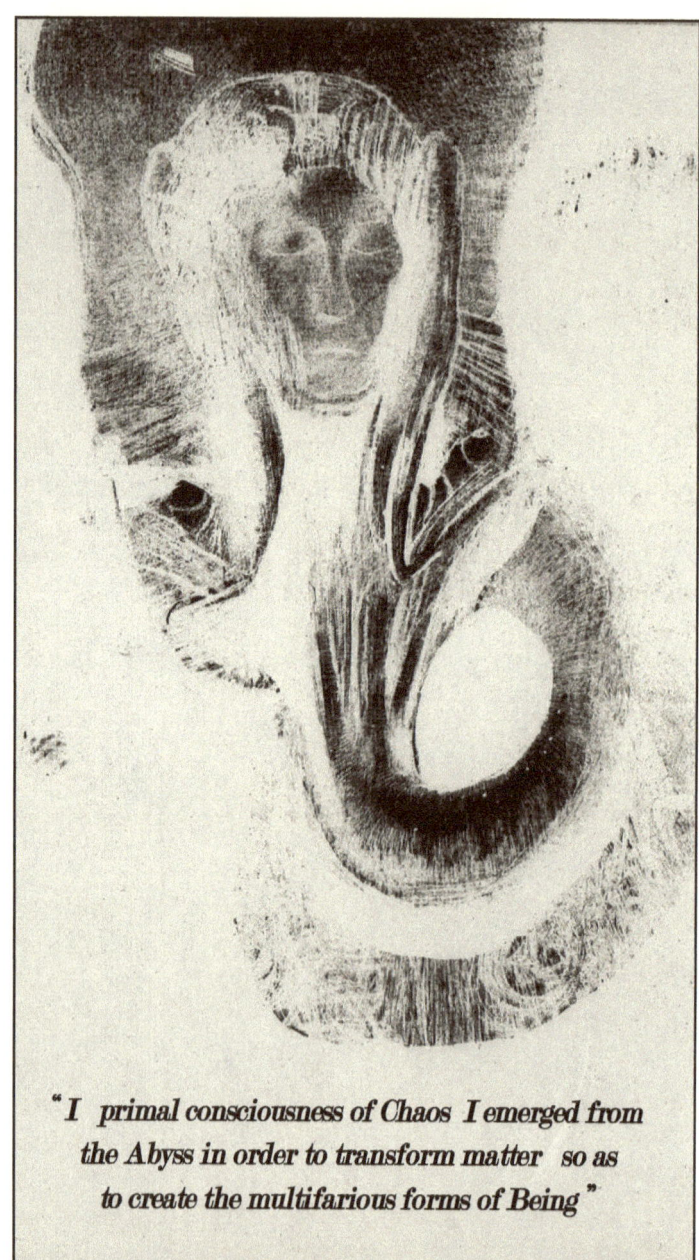

"I  primal consciousness of Chaos  I emerged from
the Abyss in order to transform matter   so as
to create the multifarious forms of Being"

## EDOUARD d'ARAILLE - POETRY WORKS

UNBORN TOMORROW: MEMORIES OF THE FUTURE (1998)

EVEN WE ARE IN ARCADIA — A VERSE CYCLE (1999)

IN A SHORT SPACE OF TIME [DÉBUT POETRY VOLUME] (1999)

OUT OF THESE EYES — A MODERN OMAR KHAYÁM (1999)

GROUND ZERO: OO/OO/OO [THE BLUE EDITION] (2000)

THE LOST VERSE — FRAGMENTS OF 'ARKADIA NUOVA' (2001)

AFTER THE FIRE: THE POET OF THE PLATEAU (2001)

NO/NSENSE — VIEWS FROM THE BORDERLAND [EDITOR] (2002)

POESIA NUEVA: THE MAN OF STONE & OTHER VERSE (2002)

MANUSCRIPT REMAINS — OF SOMA AMRITAH (2003)

THE POETRY OF LIVING TIME [ESSAYIST/EDITOR] (2003)

THE COMPLETE POETIC WORKS OF SOMA AMRITAH (2006)

GROUND ZERO: OO/OO/OO [POST 09/11 EDITION] (2007)

WORDS CAN'T HOLD... A DECADE OF POETRY (2008)

NOW OR NEVER — A POETIC ULTIMATUM (2011)

LOVE ME WHEN I DIE *WORDS FROM BEYOND THE GRAVE* (2014)

LOVE IMMORTAL: LA POÉSIE DE L'AMOUR (2015)

THE FALLEN — POETRY OF WAR, LOVE AND LOSS (2016)

OUT OF THE GHETTO : VERSE OF DISILLUSION & DESPAIR (2017)

W.M.D. — WORDS OF MASS DESTRUCTION (2017)

WORDS CAN'T HOLD... TWO DECADES OF POETRY (2018)

ADAPA'S ASCENT — A MYTH OF MAN & IMMORTALITY (2019)

JE SUIS POËTE : DAMNÉ PAR LES DIEUX (2021)

THIS IS MY PRAYER — WORDS OF A BELIEVER (2023)

BOOK OF JESUS: VOLUME ONE (2024) [TRANSLATION]

*Find the Author Online*

GREAT WORLD BOOKS ™
COLLECTION - VOL # 1

# ADAPA's ASCENT

## A Myth of Man & IMMORTALITY

"Certainly the Art of Writing is the most miraculous of all things man has devised. Odin's Runes were the first form of the work of a Hero; Books' written words are still miraculous Runes, the latest form! - In Books lies the soul of the whole Past Time; the articulate audible voice of the Past, when the body and material substance of it has altogether vanished like a dream. Mighty fleets and armies, harbors and arsenals, vast cities, high-domed, many-engined, — they are precious, great: but what do they become? Agamemnon, the many Agamemnons, Pericleses, and their Greece; all is gone now to some ruined fragments, dumb mournful wrecks and blocks: but the Books of Greece! There Greece, to every thinker, still very literally lives: can be called up again into life. No magic Rune is stranger than a Book. All that Mankind has done, thought, gained or been : it is lying as in magic preservation in the pages of Books. **They are the chosen possession of men.**"

THOMAS CARLYLE

PUBLISHED BY

This Publication is set in
Modern No.20 Typeface

www.ingramcontent.com/pod-product-compliance
Lightning Source LLC
Chambersburg PA
CBHW060556030726
47498CB00005B/1409